# LIFE DURING WARTIME

*a novel*

Katie Rogin

MASTODON

PUBLISHING

Cover art: Laura Brown
Interior design by Ali Chica

"Gimme Shelter" Written by Mick Jagger and Keith Richards. Published by ABKCO Music, Inc. Used by Permission. All rights reserved.

Copyright ©2018 by Katie Rogin

Library of Congress Cataloging-in-Publication Data

ISBN: 978-1-936196-86-9
Library of Congress Catalog Number: 2018930955

Mastadon Publishing
www.mastadonpublishing.com
Winston-Salem, North Carolina

For special discounted bulk purchases, please contact:
Mastadon Publishing sales@mastadonpublishing.com
Contact info@mastadonpublishing.com to book events, readings and author signings.

Sing in me, Muse, and through me tell the story
of that man skilled in all ways of contending,
the wanderer, harried for years on end,
after he plundered the stronghold
on the proud height of Troy,

                                  He saw the townlands
and learned the minds of many distant men,
and weathered many bitter nights and days
in his deep heart at sea, while he fought only
to save his life, to bring his shipmates home.

**"The Odyssey" by Homer**
**Translated by Robert Fitzgerald**


Yeah, a storm is threatenin'
My very life, today
And if I don't get some shelter
Lord, I'm gonna fade away

War, children, yeah
It's just a shot away, it's just a shot away
War, children, yeah
It's just a shot away, it's just a shot away, yeah

**"Gimme Shelter"**
**Mick Jagger & Keith Richards**

# Table of Contents

# AFTER MEMORY

# ONE

Jim Wicklow was swimming in his sleep. For weeks he'd been having the dream. He was swimming in an indoor pool, in a basement, a low ceiling and little light. It seemed, after he woke, around three a.m., that he had been swimming in the dark, a flashlight beam swinging across his lane. It wasn't around three though, it was precisely at 3:14 that he woke—the same time he'd woken on the mornings of September 12th, 13th and 14th seven years before. At the time he had decided it was the F-16s crossing the sound barrier as they did their flyovers, the Mach 1 boom waking him. Now, he thought maybe the waking was a wartime habit returning. But it also felt like a warning. And now he was swimming in his sleep, swimming quickly up out of sleep, because the phone was ringing.

"Oh—hi, Jim. Sorry. I thought I dialed Sarah's cell."

Jim murmured nonsense softly into the receiver, which he let drop to the pillow by his head. A heavy weight reached across him, rested on his chest, and snatched away the intruding phone, relieving him of the responsibility of being awake.

"Babe, I got it. Go back to sleep."

He rolled toward Sarah, but she slipped from his embrace before he got his arms fully around her. He'd wanted to make love to her, but she was gone. He eased into the warm place she had left in the soft sheets. He had never opened his eyes.

Jim stood in the kitchen, smelling the coffee Sarah had made for him and dumbly staring at a half bagel sitting among crumbs on the counter. He thought of it as a bad bagel and vowed not to enjoy it even as he shoved it into the toaster. Moving out of New York had meant certain sacrifices and apparently they all involved food. And tap water. Jim had called Poland Spring of Cape Cod two days after they had arrived and told them to keep the bottle deliveries coming.

The bagel popped in the middle of him pouring coffee and he paused for a moment, unsure of his priorities. He finished filling the mug, stirred in two spoonfuls of Splenda and a splash of something he assumed was milk despite the word "soy" on the carton. He grabbed the bagel and stuck it between his teeth as he conducted a two-handed search in the fridge for something to spread on it. All he found was peanut butter.

Jim used his knee to slide first the heavy glass and then the light screen door along their tracks. He emerged out onto the deck to survey his domain. He stood barefoot, sipping his coffee and nibbling with diminishing curiosity the peanut buttered bad bagel. The pond—which everyone not from Cape Cod would call a big fucking lake—was quiet this morning. Boats tied to docks, no swimmers, only a few birds. Away from the shore there was a series of what he called "plips"—gentle focused disturbances that caused circles of ripples that looked like radar readouts on submarines. It was as if someone under water was skimming a rock along the surface of the pond from below. He assumed it had something to do with fish.

He had four acres and the house. All-in, the lot with the house, the empty one next door and the lot with the teardown on the other side, had cost him one-point-four-five in cash. It was a good deal to make, but it still felt as if he had made the move too soon. He expected to be standing on his deck surveying his realm in his seventies, retired from the work-a-day, done with it all. But he stood here at fifty-two, staying busy not working, and done in by it all.

"Hey, you're up." Sarah joined him, energized and flushed from her morning run. She sucked down the contents of a water bottle. "I thought you were going to sleep in."

"I thought I did. What time is it?" Jim had stopped wearing a watch.

"Almost eight." She leaned into him, instantly drenching his T-shirt where her body touched his.

Jim still couldn't get used to how much people up here got done before breakfast. The locals even put his former Wall Street colleagues to shame, doing the most astonishing things, including a full day's work, before he rolled out of bed. And the other escapees from Boston and New York who had settled on the Cape, they burned thousands of calories running and rowing before he had finished his first cup of coffee. He was glad Sarah had embraced the lifestyle, but he would pass.

When they had first moved up here he had submitted himself to daily swimming, weightlifting and portion control—in between two AA meetings, one to start the day and the other to end it. He had lost forty pounds of fat and replaced them with ten pounds of new muscle and a slowly healing liver. This sweat-lodge phase of his self-cure had been over for a year now and he had relaxed into an easy routine. He had never been in better shape, even when he was in his twenties, riding the bond desk at Prudential Bache, a junior master of the universe who never left his chair except for his pre-dinner four-mile run.

He was only slightly embarrassed now to find himself occasionally turned on by his own body. In the warmer months he liked to jerk off in the outdoor shower, feeling free and never wanting to put clothes on again, hoping he wouldn't be interrupted so he could be alone with himself. Once, the UPS guy had steered his truck down the winding drive to the house during one of Jim's shower sessions. Jim had continued stroking away, assuming that whatever Sarah had ordered from J. Crew did not require a signature.

"Oh, and we're out of butter and cream cheese." Jim slid his hand to his wife's damp ass, grabbing a handful of jogging short.

"We don't eat butter or cream cheese."

"Since when?"

"Over a year, probably."

Jim could tell Sarah was trying to suppress great laughter. She loved these conversations where he was revealed to be either elderly or distracted or both.

"What have I been putting on bagels then?"

"Babe, you don't eat bagels. You've been an egg-whites-and-tortilla man since we left New York."

Jim stared at her, wondering if he should be more serious about this kind of thing.

"Do you think it's early Alzheimer's or something?"

"No, it's not early Alzheimer's or something." Sarah smiled the words at him. "But if it is, Jane Brody says crossword puzzles and sex are the cure."

Jim put both hands on Sarah's ass, pulling her fully to him now. "Jane Brody of the august *New York Times*?"

Sarah moved her hands around to Jim's back and placed them just below his shoulder blades. "The one and only. Crossword puzzles and sex delay dementia."

"Well, it's Monday and I don't think a Monday puzzle will do the trick, do you?" Jim tilted his head down and kissed a carefully selected portion of skin on Sarah's neck.

"It's Friday. Better make it both." Sarah pushed away from him and in very few moves removed her running clothes, dropping them to the wood planks at their feet. She stood before him in the open air—naked lean muscle sheathed in moist, gently tanned skin.

It was this kind of gesture, this confidence about her body and its effect on him, that had made Jim mistake her for a pro when they first met. He would never tell her, but he assumed, not that she was a call girl, but that she was one of those women guys like him would set up in an apartment in some building Trump owned on a high floor with crazy views and stainless steel appliances. She had such poise about the things he found foreign that he assumed she had learned them deliberately in order to hold up her end of transactions. He quickly discovered, without any embarrassing moments involving cash left on a bedside table, that she was simply another kind of woman—one from that place that an Irish guy from Brooklyn could only think of as Blonde.

"Has the Alzheimer's made you forget what to do with a naked woman?" It had not, so Jim took his thirty-seven-year-old second wife to the nearest lounge chair and fucked her in the open air and in full view of their neighbors across the pond.


"So what do you think? Can you taste the difference?" Sarah stood over Jim, waiting for an answer.

Jim put a forkful of the omelet she had made into his mouth and pantomimed an extravagant act of consideration.

"Be serious. Don't the eggs taste better?"

"All I'm tasting is feta cheese, spinach and something that's probably not oregano."

"It's thyme."

"Time for what?" Jim said this half-heartedly, knowing she hated puns.

"Ugh. Groan, groan. O-pun the door. So funny." Sarah flopped into the empty chair at the breakfast table. "C'mon. Don't the eggs taste better?"

"Honestly, they taste like you bought them at Stop & Shop."

"They come from your very own chickens a mere twenty yards away. They must taste better."

Jim looked toward the coop he had paid a local kid to build. He thought of the occupants as belonging to Sarah and the kooks he'd read about in the *Times* who were keeping chickens in their garden apartments in Park Slope and by their pool houses in the Hamptons. And here on Cape Cod. It was a DIY approach to sustainability that made sense as far as the math went, but it felt unclean to him somehow.

"Maybe we could do a taste test. You could blindfold me." Jim offered this as if he really meant to be helpful, but he wondered if there might be an investment opportunity he was missing.

"That's a great idea. We'll do a taste test when we get to Bill and Mark's. You're coming tomorrow, right? You said."

Yes, he had said. But a stop-and-start drive from where they were on the Cape all the way to Provincetown, even on the second Saturday after Labor Day, didn't feel like something to look forward to. In addition, Bill and Mark were probably the only near-contemporaries he knew who made him feel lacking in financial acumen. Jim sometimes found himself wondering if there was some special gay way of making money that they kept secret from straight guys like him, but this seemed absurd as every financial trick in the book always ended up getting revealed and circulated—not to mention the fact that he couldn't think what exactly gay men could see in the markets that he couldn't. Bill and Mark though always knew what was around the next corner, always reacted first, were already getting out before anyone else even knew to get in. And the things they owned—truly astonishing. He had owned similar things, but those days were gone, partly of his own volition and partly—completely and utterly—against his will. Maybe Jim would have a quiet chat with Bill or Mark, while he was getting a private tour of the nursery they were preparing for the adopted infant. Maybe Jim would fire up his screens more than the once a week he did now, check his positions more often, maybe make an extra trade, get into something he'd have to research. The market would be the same, he knew, going up and down, despite the recent cracks seen with Bear Stearns and Fannie and Freddie. A faint something pinged in his brain, but he shook it off.

"What time do you want to leave tomorrow for Provincetown?" This was Jim's way of telling Sarah that, yes, he was going with her.

"Early. They're setting up a special lunch for us at the restaurant so I can see what's not working." Sarah gave him a quick kiss on the cheek, sensing that he had only just in this moment agreed to the trip. "I'm going to shower. Can you feed our chickens, please?"

She disappeared up the stairs, the second story of the house claiming her, leaving Jim alone in the mid-morning quiet of his castle.

Jim slid his feet into a pair of old sneakers, his heels crushing down the backs. He used a metal bowl to scoop out feed from the large bag that leaned against the wall in the garage. He trudged across the yard toward the coop to face the chickens.

They were Rhode Island Reds. Sarah had researched them extensively on the web before buying the chicks. They were more resistant to disease, produced more eggs and were not as dumb as other chickens—intelligence in chickens existing in a tiny area all the way at the left of the spectrum, if the spectrum ran from inanimate object (on the left) to Stephen Hawking (on the right). When they had arrived via FedEx and Sarah pulled off the top of the box, there they were, fuzzy and alive. Sending live animals (he vaguely thought birds weren't officially animals) through the mail was something Jim knew he could never reconcile in his brain so he tried not to dwell on it.

He unhooked the various latches on the coop. The Reds' spectacular stupidity included escaping from the warmth and comfort of their shelter to search for food and freedom despite the fact he and Sarah fed and freed them daily. He swung the wire-and-wood door open and watched the chickens squawk and jive their way out of the coop. They were free! To do what, they did not know.

Jim watched the birds bob and weave around the grass lining the pebbly drive. He liked watching them as they tried to figure out the world. It reminded him of watching his kids when they were little, sticking things in their mouths, pushing stuff up their noses, holding large objects very close to their eyeballs. Of course, even at birth, J.J. and Emily were a thousand times smarter than the Rhode Island Reds were now.

Suddenly he felt a sharp pain on his left foot. He let out a yelp and jumped, sending the chickens into a mini fowl frenzy. There was a small remnant of a purple swoop on the sneaker. One of the chickens must have pecked at it, thinking it was something tasty. Vicious little fuckers, he thought. He spilled out the feed in an arc, letting it fall in the grass, and watched them go for it. His foot didn't hurt so much as feel violated, and his pulse raced from the surprise.

Before September 11th he had loved the thrill of a woman coming up behind him and placing her hands over his eyes and saying "guess who." And he had warmed to the screams of "Happy Birthday" as a room went from dark to light for a surprise party. But since that day, he preferred predictability, no sudden moves and consistent lighting. Even a minor out-of-the-blue attack from an idiot chicken would now stay with him for the rest of the day. He would most likely need a meeting before they left for Provincetown.

Jim watched his new enemies eat. There was enough feed for all the chickens so there was no in-fighting, no survival-of-the-fittest behavior on display, but Jim was reluctant to find human lessons in nature anyway. Wall Street wasn't the dog-eat-dog jungle people described it as. That was an outsider's take. Insiders knew the Street was fast and crowded, but guys weren't trying to kill each other, they were trying to beat the market itself into submission. Sure, there were losers when others won—and that felt fleetingly good to Jim when he was on the right side of that—but they were all trying to defy the invisible hand, smack it out of the way so they could get what they wanted, and then get more of it. Watch, wait, move, move now. Do it again. Do it faster. Do it for now and do it for a year from now. See the hand, nudge it aside, make a move, see the hand again. That's not how chickens operated. They couldn't see the hand that fed them, or the one that killed them.

Sarah had wanted to know what the birds tasted like. She thought she might want to sell them to some of the restaurants she consulted for or at least use them to help her make recommendations about feed options, free-range conditions and other things that could make menus better or at least more promotable. She researched the best way to kill the chickens, but after warily circling the coop with a sharpened knife, she had given up and returned to the kitchen complaining to Jim.

"I should be able to do this. I talk about this all the time to my clients. I'm a fraud."

Jim could see both sides of Sarah's dilemma, but ultimately he preferred that his wife not have blood on her hands.

"I read where we can put them in a Glad bag and tie them to the exhaust pipe of the car. It's less of a shock than beheading." Jim offered this both as a deterrent to Sarah's plan for chicken-cide and as a viable alternative to the knife. But Sarah had just looked at him, pleading for him to solve this for her.

"I'll call someone. We'll have someone do it for us." He had thought this would make her feel better.

"I'm a failed foodie." She wailed, dropped the knife on the table and fled to their bedroom.

Jim had thought she was kidding at first, but realized quickly that he better take this seriously. After he found the right guy and made the arrangements on the phone, he stood at the bottom of the stairs, yelling up to her as if cajoling J.J. or Emily to come back downstairs and finish their Brussels sprouts.

"We'll watch him and learn how it's done." Silence from upstairs. "He's an experienced, trained expert in this. He'll teach us and we'll learn. And then you'll be an experienced, trained expert and you can do it yourself." More silence. "It's okay not to know everything all the time. That's why they call it learning." Sarah had come stomping down the stairs then.

"But I say I know everything and it turns out I don't."

Welcome to the world, he remembered thinking.

Now, watching the remaining chickens peck at what was left of their feed, Jim wondered what he had been talking about. He suspected his world was at a standstill. He'd been hiding out now for seven years. He only occasionally peeked at his screens or at the newspapers. He was all too familiar with what he called the "beforeworld"—before the buildings came down, before he lost his business, his brother and his bearings. Money didn't change, he assumed that much. If he plugged back in now, what would he find—after? What did the world offer now?

# TWO

Captain Lise Sheridan—recently discharged honorably from the 10th Combat Support Hospital, U.S. Army—knew with tremendous certainty, as she sat in a Studio City kitchen, that Danny Gold would step into the doorway to ask if she was okay because she was taking too long getting the Coke Zero out of the fridge. Danny had been asking stupid questions again. Or maybe they were just questions that were too hard to answer. She popped the top of the can deliberately, sat down at the small table and sucked at the edge of the can, all in an attempt to slow time. Lise needed these moments when she was away from other people. Other people were dangerous. The doctors at Walter Reed had said it might be like this, but what soldier, or Army nurse for that matter, ever listened to a shrink.

"Tell me about a good day in Iraq." When Danny had asked this, that now-familiar hum on the surface of Lise's skin spread across her arms and legs.

"There were no good days," she had answered him, but her voice wasn't part of her anymore.

"Tell me about a better day then."

"I thought you wanted to hear about truck and raw—I mean—" slower now, as she found the right words: "Shock and awe, carnage and mayhem."

"I need a scene at page sixty, a respite, a quiet moment when everyone, including the audience, can take a breather."

"Before the hero recommits?"

"You remembered."

"The memory comes and goes."

"Can you remember a good—a better—day?"

She spat it out quickly: "I was coming back from the gym in the Green Zone and there was a mortar attack. Nobody got hurt." This wasn't true.

"Anything else? Maybe not moving, just sitting around? Maybe you stood looking out at the horizon, the mountains maybe, and you thought of home. Maybe not mountains, but the desert?"

"Are you fucking kidding me?" This was when she finally extracted herself from the couch and made her exit to the kitchen.

There were days when Lise thought this was the worst thing she'd ever agreed to, including joining the Army during wartime. Telling a Hollywood screenwriter stories, secrets and statistics about being an Army nurse in Iraq, trying to translate her words for traumatic amputations into words he could use. And maybe the second worse thing she'd ever agreed to was to sleep with him, often just to break the tense silence between them.

The VA docs had given her a lot of acronyms and abbreviations, but in the end, it was simple: she'd been in a war zone for eighteen months and she had got hit in the head. Even in her support group—run by the annoying Nik, up in the Sierra Madre hills—she was the only one with no visible evidence of war. But they all said it was fine, no worries, Captain, you fought like us, you took care of us. You were there.

Danny twisted his upper body into the doorway, leaving his legs around the corner out of sight. "You okay?"

Lise turned away from him so he wouldn't see the little smile on her face, which only made her usually down-turned mouth look neutral instead of happy. "Just having a moment. Refueling."

"How about a little drinking down at the Moon?"

These words were the potent code between them for an extended series of intimate events. Lise swiveled to face Danny as she gave serious thought to his offer. He was suggesting they abandon the screenplay, head to his local bar, have a few drinks, return to the apartment and have slow civilian sex. She was moved by the fact he thought this would make her feel better—or even, good—and she was relieved he was giving her activities in which she wouldn't have to talk so much. The words weren't coming, or they were coming in mixed-up jumbles. The VA docs called them crazy salads and she already had a full day of them. The little girl's birthday party she had attended that afternoon had been confusing, with too many new people, too many words. She had hoped Nina would stay by her to translate, but that hadn't happened and Lise couldn't remember why.

"Sure. Sounds good." She said this with a sense that she possessed her own voice, which surprised her. Drinking always helped her say the right words.

"Let me just change my shirt," he said.

Danny disappeared to the bedroom while Lise sat feeling un-girl-like in her Army-issue T-shirt and a pair of jeans she'd borrowed from Nina. She wasn't primping for the bar, but Danny had to wear the exact right shirt to signal he was an employed, produced screenwriter who was drinking to get his lover into bed and not because he had writer's block or couldn't sell a script. It was a thing like this that made Lise think Danny was an idiot. Why couldn't he just wear what he was wearing and leave the apartment without thinking? She thought of Major Beck telling everyone to slow down, speak calmly, know you're doing the right thing—even as she was rushing-rushing with a Marine's bloody body knowing he was just seconds away from losing a limb or two. If she could just slow down time with Danny, then maybe.

Nik always said he and his Vietnam guys had talked about going back to the world when their tours were over. For them, the world was home. But when Danny took more than five minutes to decide which of his many shirts to wear, as he was doing now, Lise thought of home as a broken world. When Danny made love to her though, with his smoky single-malt breath and his large smooth hands, as he would a few hours from now, his ignorance floating away, she thought she was the one who was broken.

Lise and Danny sat at the short end of the bar. Lise leaned into the dusty posters shellacked to the wall and looked up at the television that hung over the other end of the bar. She saw uniformed people moving among the wreckage of a train crash. She couldn't tell if she was accelerating or slowing because of what she saw there. She put her hands in her lap and looked away. Danny looked to the bartender hoping to order, but the guy ignored him, drying glasses and checking levels in bottles in his speed rack. Lise leaned reluctantly toward the bartender and his wall of bottles, feeling a spotlight on her face. The guy suddenly came alive and moved toward them. Lise hoped he'd take their order from Danny, but he smiled at her.

"Hey, sister. How's it going today?"

"I'm good." Lise cleared her throat and looked away. "We're good."

"Feel like a civilian yet?"

She must have been really drunk, moved to telling stories filled with memory gaps. She hoped she hadn't boasted, but then what were war stories anyway but extended bragging. Half the bartenders in L.A. seemed to be vets of one war or another. Some were ex-hippies, some ex-G.I.'s, some both—all of them hungover or clean and sober. Lise felt at home with them, but always resisted the initial recognition and camaraderie until she yielded to it. She didn't like the way it eclipsed Danny though, with his fan of credit cards and clean shirts.

"Danny?" She looked to him, signaling the ex-soldier behind the bar exactly how she wanted this to go, reserving judgment of Danny for herself and no one else.

Danny ordered his whiskey and her beer and as the bartender faded away, Danny slipped his hand along her back, felt her tense and then sat back, keeping his hands to himself. Lise knew he was thinking that she just needed a drink.

"How much longer do you think you'll stay out here?" Danny could mistake heavy conversation for small talk.

Lise answered immediately, as if she knew for sure. "I was thinking about maybe getting a job, a nursing job. Keeping charts in a doc's office maybe. Pay is shit, but I got mad skills." If her numbness could accommodate a want of any kind at all, it was to be in an ER or on a paramedic truck on a Saturday night in some gun-ridden neighborhood. She looked at the television again. The news people sat in a studio talking to each other, very concerned.

"You don't want to go home to Denver?" He was asking if Lise was staying because she wanted to be with him.

The bartender delivered their drinks and they sipped away the tension. And then that familiar B-minor electric strum came from the speakers around them.

She'd heard the song her entire life, born two years after it was released. Her father had played it endlessly whenever his dark moods hit, bellowing to her mother about how it was the true signal the 60s had really ended. Fuck Altamont and Watergate, this—he would flap the album cover in the air—was the death knell, with dueling guitars, in our bicentennial year. But when Lise heard the song in Los Angeles, it had a freshness that surprised her, reaching a place in her that war and memory loss hadn't touched.

She could see Danny's body sway slightly to the song. Why had she so quickly agreed to meet this screenwriter? She was slow to make all other decisions except the reflexive kind. Maybe it was the weather. The light in this place was different than light she had known elsewhere—not Rocky Mountain light or Baghdad light. And the palm trees did this silhouette thing against the blue blue sky—a blue Lise knew she had never seen before except maybe in some paintings once at the Denver Art Museum. And Danny stood among these colors and shapes and when she heard the song on the radio—it must have been playing when she first met him— it made her feel close to—what? She remembered pulling into the parking lot, watching Danny step to greet her—this moment of repair, made of blue and sun and breeze and twin guitars and *the warm smell of colitas rising up through the air.* She had felt un-broken for the first time since the Green Zone attacks, since Ramstein and Walter Reed, since—when?

"No, I don't think I'll go home to Denver," she said, finally answering his question. "Let's get out of here," Lise added, leaning toward Danny, reaching to touch him, wondering if the bartender was watching and not approving.

"Now?"

Lise nodded because she had lost the words.

"I was just getting this idea, this click in my head." Danny talked and Lise lost the thread as he re-routed her away from what she had just offered. "I was thinking, what if—now hear me out— what if the unit doesn't get caught up in the deaths at the school and the private doesn't confide in the nurse. What if—" Danny droned, spinning Lise's stories back at her with differences slight and extreme, building a war tale that bore no relation to the world she knew. Had he been listening at all? She thought of calling Nina again—wondered why Nina hadn't returned her last call—thought of thanking her again for lending her the jeans, confiding in her that this guy was clueless, what was she doing with him? Nina would laugh, remind Lise she was supposed to be the older, wiser one.

"Isn't your script about the Cash?" She occupied her mouth with the beer bottle immediately after she got the words out.

"It is...Wait, you've never called it that before. Cash, like in CSH, combat support hospital?" Danny pulled his eyebrows togeth-er. "I need to write that down." He slapped at his pockets, found nothing and grabbed a BevNap from the bar stack. The bartender appeared with a pen for Danny, wiggling his nose at Lise as if writ-ers without pens on their person gave off a stench. Lise noticed her nose was wrinkled too.

Maybe telling her stories to Danny would get her back on track. Telling him about Baghdad, about treating the wounded, might give her order again. She hardly remembered anything, but somehow she was able to retrieve recollections from deep in her muscles. She felt so far away from herself even when she was telling her stories, so far from the roaring sense of purpose being an army nurse had given her. She wanted back into that.

Lise's mother was a doctor and the one thing the daughter of a doctor couldn't do was become a nurse. Her dad taught history at DU and preached from his Eames lounge chair, stabbing at guacamole with blue corn chips. Other than the Broncos, he wasn't keen on people who wore uniforms. Lise caught sight of the train wreckage on the TV screen again and thought maybe she would call her parents, talk to them, holding the phone close to her ear.

At some point, she had escalated to tequila shots with the beer and Danny had moved his bar stool so his knees were between her thighs. She leaned back into the wall and listened to him spin his tales. He wasn't behaving badly or in a way he hadn't before, but definitely in a way that would not fulfill the earlier promise of the evening. Desire was fading instead of spreading through her. She wanted out and away from him. He was too drunk now anyway.

Lise had to half-support Danny when they walked back to his apartment. The boulevard was noisy and dirty, but it was populated and seemed safe to her as they moved from too-bright spaces to too-dark ones. They turned into the murky light of residential streets and she slipped into vigilance before she realized it, checking behind them as they walked the three blocks, peering ahead and then checking behind, constantly scanning for movement. She was amped way beyond reach of the calming alcohol when she dumped him on his bed. She stood over him, watching him shudder a little as he mumbled and curled up. Lise flipped open her phone, told Nik's voicemail that she needed to talk to someone who got it, and buzz-drove the Jetta out to the Sierra Madre hills where the vets waited for her.

No one answered the bell at Nik's so Lise put her face close to the big picture window. Someone was zonked out on the couch and she could see the blue and white lights from the television ka-

leidoscope over him. The canyon around her made nature noises
and she wondered what was actually in the woods. Her heart rate
had dropped as she drove, but now it was climbing again—and she
found the erratic rhythm a relief after Danny-time. This was not a
good sign.

Nik pulled open the rough wood of the front door and
stepped out into the dark.

"Friend or foe?"

Lise walked past him and through the doorway without answering.

"Permission to enter, granted," she heard him say behind her.

Lise moved through the living room where a couple of guys—
one may have been Acevedo and another was definitely Maxwell—
were playing *Call of Duty IV*. She went into the bathroom and shut
the door. Her jeans were hanging on the shower rod where she had
left them. They had dried. She put her face to the crotch and was
relieved to find it smelled of lavender soap instead of urine. She
quickly pulled off Nina's jeans and slid into her own.

"You okay in there, Sheridan?" Nik called to her from
beyond the door.

"I'm good. Just changing back into my clothes." She opened
the door to him.

"Any thought about why you pissed your pants the other
night?" Nik could be such a shrink.

"Weak bladder?"

"If that's how you want to play it, tough guy."

Lise didn't want to do this right now although she knew eventually she would have to have a Nik session. Group talking was one
thing, but his war veteran self-help guru magic really came out in
what he called sessions—marathon one-on-ones where he helped
you with your shit in allegedly epic ways, got you straight, got you
spiritually on the mend so you could make a life. You had to come
back for tune-ups and weekly groups were always good, but after a
Nik session, vets could deal. At least that's what he advertised. Lise
was of two or three minds on Nik and his ways, but she did suspect
that Nik's hillside held more wisdom than Danny and his crowd.

"You seen Nina?" Lise wanted to return the jeans.

"Haven't seen her, but I think she left her backpack in the kitchen."

"But she usually has it with her. It's got all her stuff in it."

"It's here, she's not. What can I tell you?"

## THREE

$L$ise woke up sure she knew where she was only to realize she was mistaken. She smelled Denver and then the Green Zone, as if her nose was switching channels. Then she smelled cooking bacon and her location came to her: Major Beck's family's apartment above the garage, Sierra Madre, CA, 91025.

After her visit to Nik's the night before, she had headed out intending to drive all the way back to Danny's in Studio City, banging on his door, waking him up. But as she came down from the canyon and passed Nina's street she had taken a right, circling the block and pulling up along the curb. The main house where Nina's landlady and her family lived was lit up. Lise could see the party decorations still on the walls. Why didn't people clean up after themselves? Lise couldn't remember where Nina had gone after the party or maybe Nina hadn't said. From the car Lise could see to the rear of the lot where Nina's rental house sat. That house was dark. Lise and Nina had been talking about her moving out of Major Beck's and into the other bedroom at Nina's. The stillness of Nina's place seemed something more than uninviting. Lise had felt warned off. She had moved her foot from the brake pedal to the gas and driven straight to Major Beck's. Danny probably wouldn't wake until morning.

She had slept most of the night, which surprised her—she usually only slept once she was sure the sun was coming up. She was glad not to wake at Danny's where his early morning industry made her feel grumpy and hung over even when she wasn't.

Lise lay under the sheet wondering if she could breathe away her morning anxiety. Maybe if she just skipped the shower she wouldn't have the attack. She thought the word "steak" instead of "attack" and immediately pictured a large breakfast on a table in front of her: meat, eggs, toast, potatoes, orange juice, coffee. She thought of diners, Formica tabletops, aprons with stains. The bacon smell pulled her from the bed, but she wasn't hungry. It was simply time to start another day.

Lise would connect with Nina today. She would make an effort to do that, if she could find the sustained will. She would make the rounds of the usual places—where they drank, where they talked, where they sat in silence. She would speak to the people they knew—Jen the landlady, that guy Nina had been maybe sleeping with unless he'd gone back to Afghanistan. She would go to Nik's again—tear Maxwell and Acevedo away from the joy stick, make Nik pay attention even when Lise barely could. She didn't have the energy to be concerned, she told herself, she just wanted to see her new friend, her new friend who hadn't returned three voicemail messages, who had left her backpack where she wasn't, who hadn't been seen since—when?

She stared at the shower stall, the dread rising in the lower region of her throat as she knew it would. She bathed in the sink, cupping water from the faucet in her palms and splashing it awkwardly into her armpits and between her legs. There were puddles of water all over the tiled floor when she finished and she was careful not to slip as she reached for the towel. *Iraq War Veteran Dies in U.S. Bathroom.* She saw the headline, but couldn't tell if it was the *Denver Post* or another paper. It didn't scare her, it just made her feel stupid. Most everything else scared her—*that* she could remember. She needed to get certified in something new, get a job, save some lives. She needed to actually feel something other than fear. For now she would lie down on the unmade bed—until the dizziness passed, until the electrical firing in her brain stopped. Then she would look for Nina.

The rental house was empty. Lise didn't knock, didn't hope Nina would answer the door. She knew Nina wasn't there so she just walked inside.

The house was still and dusty. The windows were open, but everything was in its place. The kitchen and bathroom were spotless. Shampoos, conditioners and moisturizers were lined up in a neat row. A frying pan and a dish stood in the drying rack. The bed was made and Nina's clothes were put away neatly in the closet and the drawers of the wooden bureau. A messenger bag from New York hung on the knob of the closet door. Lise looked under the bed and found nothing. She pulled the edge of the spread down, smoothing the fabric in place, and sat up on her knees. The hooked rug carpet made a raggedy circle under her. She couldn't remember what she was supposed to be thinking.

"Mommy's in her bedroom," the little girl said when she opened the door to Lise.

"Why are you opening the door to a stranger?" Lise didn't know how to talk to children.

"You're Captain Lise. You're Nina's friend. You were at my party."

"I could be anybody."

"But you're Lise."

"I forgot your name."

"It's okay, you don't have to be sorry. Mommy forgets stuff all the time." Lise waited. "My name is Mia."

The conversation had clearly run its course so Lise stepped into the house and closed the door behind her. The little girl was wearing a kind of plastic basket on her back that held plastic arrows and the thing that shot arrows. Lise couldn't think of the words for these objects.

Mia indicated that Lise should bend down and lean in close to hear her whisper. Lise didn't like being this close to a small person. What if she pushed her by accident? She'd break into a million pieces. Mia cupped a hand around the side of her mouth and Lise reluctantly moved her ear into the warmth of the little girl's palm.

"Mommy got in bed in the middle of my party. She won't come out." They both straightened up and Mia pointed toward the back of the house. In full voice Mia announced, "Daddy said he was fuck piss."

"You mean, fucking pissed?" Lise asked.

Mia nodded very seriously, allowing herself to say the grown-up words only once. And then she fled, bare feet slapping on the wood floors, toward where she had pointed. The arrows made a muted rattling sound as she moved. Lise didn't think she had gone to her mother's room.

Lise heard Jen call from the bedroom.

"It's Lise Sheridan. Is this a good time for a visit?" Lise shouted back. She thought she heard Jen say something like come back to the bedroom, but Lise didn't want to venture any further into other people's private spaces. Looking through Nina's place had been enough. She stood in the living room for a moment, realized she'd been holding her breath and let it out in a slow exhale. She breathed deeply in and out again and then walked toward Jen's voice.

Lise hesitated at the bedroom door. It was partially closed and she dreaded what she would find on the other side.

"Lise, is that you? Come on in. I'm dressed." Jen's voice came from behind the door.

Lise pushed herself through the doorway and over the threshold into the room. Jen lay on top of the made bed, propped up against several pillows. She wore two shirts layered over each other and jeans and navy suede Pumas.

"Sorry to greet you like the Queen, but I just needed to lie down. Kind of having a bad day."

"You wear shoes in bed?" Lise couldn't help but ask the question.

"Kind of having a bad week, if you know what I mean. What if I have to leave all of a sudden? So the sneakers are on."

This conversation seemed reasonable to Lise, but she didn't like standing over the woman on the bed. It reminded her of hovering over bloodied prone bodies, military and civilian, in all the places where she had seen the injured.

"Did Nina lock herself out again?" Jen asked.

"Nina's not around. I'm looking for her."

Jen sat up, triggered by something in Lise's flat tones. "Weren't you at the party together?"

"I'm sorry I left early." Or maybe Nina had been the one to leave first.

"Oh please. I left early myself—and I'm the mom. Twelve seven-year-olds is dealable, but their parents are another story. Especially if you run out of adult beverages. The juice-box mafia will turn on you in a heartbeat."

Lise didn't really know what the woman was talking about. "You didn't see Nina after the party?"

"You sound like a detective movie."

"She hasn't picked up her messages, hasn't returned calls. She's probably off on a lost weekend with what's-his-name. It's not a big deal."

"What is his name?" Jen had a worried look on her face—a look that Lise's face should have matched.

"Sergeant something." Lise couldn't really remember what the guy looked like. "I'll check the house again, if that's okay. I have a key."

"Wait. Let me give you her mother's number—I don't know why—just in case."

Jen rolled toward one of the bedside tables. She retrieved an Apple phone like Danny had just bought, a pad of paper and a pen.

"Here." Jen handed Lise the paper. "Her name is Diana Wicklow. Call her. Maybe Nina told her where she was going, if she went somewhere." Lise stared down at the piece of paper, the name and number scrawled across it, legible and threatening. If she took the information, it meant she might use it, which meant she thought Nina was in trouble, which meant she was in trouble herself. "She's cool. It's okay," Jen added.

Lise grabbed the paper and left. She walked out of the room, down the hallway and straight to Mia's room.

Lise blundered in, disturbing carefully placed toys. Mia sat on the floor amid a plastic population of small animals and people. She still wore the basket of arrows. The little girl said nothing, just folded her legs and held them to her chest. She kept her eyes open.

Lise bent down, crushing horses and firemen, and lifted the skirt of the bedspread. She thrust her head under the bed. There was more empty dusty space, like at Nina's. She turned her head to the little girl.

"There're no monsters there, Captain Lise."

Lise exhaled and lay her head down on the floor to rest. Maybe she could just lie there for a few minutes.

Lise checked the rental house again. This time she found Nina's phone. It was lying shut and silent in the drawer of the bedside table, a place she hadn't thought to look before. Why was it here? Lise opened the phone. The locked display told her there were seven messages waiting. She shut the phone in her palm. It made such a satisfying sound as it sprung close, but she couldn't help but feel that Nina was locked away behind the display, inside the plastic and wires.

Lise sat in the Sierra Madre police station and stared into her empty hands. No obvious tools of any trade, just creases and calluses and a scar on her right thumb from failing to master an old sewing machine when she was twelve. The detective sitting at his desk across from her had a gun in a holster at his belt. As he did his paperwork, pulled things from drawers, and reached for the phone, she could see the holster shift position to fit his moving body. Guns were everywhere.

In Iraq each day, at the Daily Morning Report, Lise had to show her pistol to the people who keep track of these things. It was just to make sure the doctors and nurses hadn't lost their weapons since they refused to walk around with them strapped to their bodies. For some of the medical staff it was an important point to make about the difference between them and the soldiers on both sides. For others it was a way to pretend that they were still at home, like the pirated cable in their residences and the golf clubs leaning against the wall and the rooftop cigar parties. Almost every doctor and nurse Lise knew was relieved to give up their weapon when they were discharged. Lise had unloaded and cleaned the pistol the way she had been trained and handed it, grip first, to the discharge sergeant. As the metal left her hands she felt that slight tremor when priorities are restored and worlds right themselves.

"What else do you need from me?" Lise reached for her Colorado driver's license on the detective's desk.

"Just a few more minutes." He watched her slide the license closer. "Sure, you can have that back. Oh, and I'll notify the VA. They like to know this kind of thing for their records."

"I bet." Lise hadn't meant to make a face when she said this, but it happened anyway.

"This is a favor for Nik," the detective explained. "He helped me, I help his—and you. And this Nina Wicklow. Usually, as you know from all that television you watch, this is way too soon to file a report. But given the circumstances this'll be more than a missing persons thing pretty fast."

"She's not dead." Lise said it as a fact not an argument. "It's only been a couple of hours." Another almost-fact.

The detective looked at her, not with pity but with another fact. "It's been over night. And you're here."

Yeah whatever, Lise thought. "She doesn't have a gun anymore."

The detective shook his head from side to side like what was he going to do with these kids today. "Easy to remedy."

"She's just missing," Lise said, as if she was reading an item on a menu to a waiter.

"I can get you someone to talk to. A counselor. Other than Nik, if you want."

"That's okay." She dropped her eyes to the floor. "It's all the same."

Lise leaned back in the chair, realizing she was gaining energy from all this. It wasn't taking anything from her, it wasn't making her weary as she thought it should have. She was raring to go. She slipped into her speedy hyper-tasking mode, doing her super-competent 360 thinking, sensing everything keenly, people neutralized and objects coming alive as allies. "Will you call her mom?"

The detective looked at the paper in front of him. "Diana Wicklow, New York area code?" He shifted his gaze to Lise who immediately looked away. "I think I'll hold off for a few more hours. Maybe we'll have something to tell her."

"You have my cell?"

"Yes, Sheridan. I have your number."

"You'll call me when you know something?"

"I'll call you when I know something. You do the same?"

Lise sat in the Jetta for a long time in the parking lot of the police station. She didn't want to go to Nik's. Even though he had cleared the way for her to talk to the detective, he would still be angry that she had gone to someone else for help. She didn't want to go home to Major Beck's. He was just a little too chill about everything sometimes. Lise wanted to indulge in the rushing-rush emergency she was experiencing. That meant she would go to Danny's—drink, fuck, roar to loud music, then re-pack it all into a nicely wrapped gift of imprecisely told stories he could use in his screenplay, stories that didn't hold.

Even preparing herself ahead of time didn't make it easier for Lise to be with people—especially Danny, who always ended up with all of him inside all of her. And this time what she had prepared for did not happen and she felt alarmingly disconnected from the world.

He wanted to write. She could drink, she could talk, she could shout over the music, but he was going to write while she did all this and she couldn't touch him until he was done.

Drinking alone was one thing, but drinking while someone else didn't wasn't exactly Lise's idea of a good time, especially as she was trying to tamp down this rising bad voodoo energy from her bad day. She needed a partner in crime and Danny wanted an official source. Danny wanted blood and guts and heroism and administrative details to keep it all real and prove he'd done his research with a real live witness. All Lise could see was Nina in bad places. All Lise wanted was to obliterate those images.

"Lise. You need to focus for me. Does this make sense? Let me read this and please listen. Would it happen like this?" Danny read, trying to change his voice for different characters and the stage directions. He conjured no new images for her so she listened harder, but what he said was not what she heard. Her mind spasmed and a tremor of terror went through her limbs. Should she run to somewhere where she understood what was going on?

Lise's brain replayed a fabricated Nina movie loop: a series of images of Nina in every bad place she'd likely ever been, somewhere not safe, but not too far from sanctuary. Lise saw California colors and shapes, mashed them to colors and shapes from Iraq, and tried to feel—pain, grief, a sense of urgency, anything. But the numbness asserted itself with calm resolve.

"What do you think?" Danny looked at her expectantly.

"I think that's probably about right. People call each other by their names and nicknames a lot and their ranks. So maybe you want to do that some more." She hadn't heard a word he had read to her.

"I think that's called direct address. Like if I said, I think that's called direct address, Lise. Or, what do you think, Captain? Is that what you mean, Lise?" He wasn't smiling enough for her to be absolutely sure he was being funny on purpose.

"That's exactly what I mean, Danny." She smiled too. Making stuff up for the movies was more fun than lying in real life.

Danny closed his laptop, a good day's work behind him.

"What were you thinking for dinner?" Danny asked.

Lise had stopped at Starbucks before she had walked over to the police station. She'd had a *venti* something she couldn't remember and crunched on a caramel-tasting thing she thought was called a biscotti. That, and the beer she was drinking, had been her sustenance for the day so far.

Danny sat by her on the couch and she felt crowded.

She stood up and pulled out her phone.

"I need to make a call."

"Sure. I'll change my shirt while you do that and then we'll go get something to eat. I know, no sushi. Too complicated." Danny vanished from the room.

Lise fished the paper out of her jeans, uncrumpled it to find the name and number still legible. When Nina's mother answered the phone, she sounded groggy, but Lise remembered she'd been an ER nurse, maybe still was, and assumed her hands were already moving efficiently despite being half-asleep.

Lise talked, said official things, asked if the Sierra Madre detective had called her. Danny appeared in the doorway and she slipped into another mode, dropping the filters, losing herself a little as she explained who she was to Nina's mother and why she was worried.

"Will you come find her?" she asked before she hung up. Nina's mother was maybe still talking, she wasn't sure.

Danny stepped to her, but stopped a few feet away, sensing there was a perimeter he shouldn't cross.

"You know Nina?" Lise looked at Danny's laptop, lying on the table, quietly folded, holding all its information.

"How's she doing?"

"Nina's gone."

Danny opened his mouth, then quickly shut it, sensing something else intruding. "Dead gone?"

Lise shut her eyes. Did she have to explain everything to him?

# FOUR

Jim was sleeping and yet knew something terrible was happening somewhere beyond sleep. He tore himself from slumber and awoke to the couch and a screaming television. CNN was shouting impending doom for a slutty mom with a lost and likely dead child in Florida. At least the world wasn't ending.

It took him a few sweaty seconds too long to reassemble the evening. He thought he'd had a drink. He could see himself in the clothes he was wearing now, sitting on the couch where he was sitting, holding a thick glass of something clear and cold, a lemon slice wedged between ice cubes. He could almost taste it, feel its calming chill as it went through him. It was like those dreams ex-smokers told him about—they're so real they have to sniff their clothes when they wake up in the morning. But he hadn't had a drink, he'd just wanted one very badly.

He hadn't gone to a meeting even though he had told Sarah numerous times throughout the afternoon that this was his after-dinner plan. He had paced, restless, keeping his back to the walls as he moved through the house. Going upstairs seemed an impossible feat so when Sarah had gone up to read in bed, he had stayed in the living room with the television for companionship. He had stared out into the dark beyond the window screens, thinking about getting in the car, driving to the church, sitting in whatever meeting was going on. But the outside world seemed too scary to him and so he had simply turned up the volume on the newsy hysteria.

Sarah wouldn't be upset about his having spent the night on the couch. She knew there were events that clung to him, gripped him from inside and hung on until he could shake them loose. He had slept with the lights on, slept on the floor beside their bed, slept sitting up in a chair in the kitchen, slept half-sitting in the threshold of the front door holding a baseball bat—as well as a few nights on the couch, CNN's ticker crawl pulling his eyelids down until he could sleep.

He didn't want Sarah's pitying morning looks so he slipped into his chicken-feeding sneakers and got in his car. There was a six a.m. meeting for newbies still sick-drunk from the night before and hardcore old timers who couldn't get through the night. He drove in the misty brightening light, taking quick whiffs of his pits to see if he smelled.

Jim got the nod from the meeting leader as he filled his ceramic mug with awful coffee. The AA rooms had gone green: no more Styrofoam cups, which had previously masked the dreadful brew with plastic creakiness. There were a few merchant marine types doing some heavy milling at the back of the room. He was sure they'd been dry for decades, but they all still looked like drinkers, teetering on their feet with liquid eyes and over-moist lips.

Jim took a seat as far from other people as he could manage without looking like he was in trouble. AA had been a useful tool, but Jim didn't buy it all. He needed a rigorous plan in 2004 to get his shit together and the program suited his purpose. He didn't do the steps or accept offers from men who wanted to be his sponsor, he just worked the program his way by not drinking and by showing up to a meeting as often as was necessary. He didn't share his story, but he listened closely to the others. He had shrugged when Sarah asked if he wanted her to go to an Al-Anon meeting. He thought of his drinking as a reasonable response to what he had experienced, but it was no way to live. This was why he had stopped. Living sober still meant days and nights worrying that fear lay in wait to grip him from within, but he would figure out how to deal with it—but it would not be on someone else's schedule or with someone else's rules.

"Is this seat taken?"

Jim stared at the intruder, a tall, twenty-something kid around J.J.'s age, likely spending the summer washing dishes before heading back for his senior year. He didn't look like one of those shitbag, over-eager types who had an internship every summer at a law firm or bank. He looked settled and confident as if his tech start-up had already financed his life and his descendants for generations to come, but he was keeping it real with a crappy summer job on the Cape. Maybe he was in love.

Jim gestured with an upturned palm to the maybe twenty empty seats around the room. "None of those look good to you?"

The kid sat a chair away from Jim and stretched out his indecently long legs so his battered sneakers rested on a chair two rows in front of them. "Too many empty parking places. It's hard to choose."

Jim smiled because he often said the same thing, but he didn't want to make a friend this morning so he shut himself down and broke the connection between them.

The leader began the meeting and it took on its usual rhythm and ritual. Jim listened to a few stories that had no meaning for him. He drifted, felt himself re-assembling, getting clear and feeling intact despite the night of bad sleep. The kid next to him stood and Jim tuned back in.

"Hi, my name is Mike and I'm an alcoholic." The room mumbled back at him.

Mike didn't reveal much except that he was older than Jim had thought and after almost five years sober he had slipped. He had slipped in a completely innocuous way, not paying attention to warning signs, not taking care, believing he had it under control and could take his eye off the ball. It could've happened to anyone, he said, anyone who hadn't realized the thing was still there.

"I'm Mike and I'm one day sober." The kid sat down, looking stockier to Jim, vibrating somehow, not so long and lean and world-easy.

Jim couldn't get away from the kid and the meeting fast enough. He left before the Serenity Prayer, before he'd have to take the kid's hand and recite the lines. Keep coming back because it works. No it didn't, Jim thought as he started up the car. This is bullshit, he insisted as he turned onto the main road. See the hand, push it aside, beat the market. By the time he pulled into his driveway, Jim wanted nothing more than to be clean and whole and in charge, and he hoped it was just within reach.

He slid into the driver's seat as Sarah closed the trunk on their bags. When she got in beside him she took a moment to smooth out her skirt under her thighs, lifting herself off the seat and sweeping the flowing fabric into place. Jim liked watching this gesture, his wife arranging herself in the world.

"You sure you want to drive?" She reached for the radio dial as she said this, knowing the answer, not needing to hear it.

"I'm good. And I promise no road rage when we hit traffic."

"You'll just mutter 'motherfucker' under your breath."

"You know me well, wife of wine."

"That's funny. Wife of wine."

Jim laughed and smiled with her as he started the car, but he hadn't heard his own misspoken word. Had he really said wine instead of mine? What was it called? Not dementia but—aphasia, that was it. Something new to worry about.

"Freudian slip?" Sarah asked, as he turned the car out of the driveway.

"Something like that," Jim said. "Can you find a little classic rock on that, please?" He nodded toward the radio. "It'll get us there faster."

Two hours later they were just approaching Provincetown. Jim had averaged about thirty miles and six motherfuckers per hour, but he felt refreshed instead of beaten and he and Sarah popped out of the car with energy after the wheels finally crunched the pebbly drive at Bill and Mark's. They were welcomed with hugs from the couple who smelled like vanilla and salt water. Bill offered Sarah a tour of his newly renovated kitchen while Mark took Jim out to the deck for the view of the beach and water beyond that he knew gave Jim special relief.

"Jesus fucking Christ. Every single time I'm here, I can't believe you see this every morning." Jim leaned his forearms on the thick wood railing and inhaled with his nose and his eyes. This was a domain to behold: wild water stretching forever and then crashing to smooth sand almost right in front of the house. The ocean seemed alive as if it were an enormous creature writhing and undulating in constant motion, rising and falling, breathing. Jim felt nothing for the plips in the pond he had left behind.

"Morning, noon and night. You and Sarah can have it too. I'm sure you can make someone along the beach an offer."

"Not sure I'd trust myself to not grow tired of it. Know what I mean?" Jim stared out into the water, not really expecting Mark to answer.

"We're glad you came with Sarah today." This made Jim look into Mark's face.

"Is this visit more than about her helping with your restaurant project?"

Mark smiled broadly as if to say he was unarmed and Jim could pat him down if he wanted to make sure. "We've all talked about it, but I wanted to be the one to ask you."

"Much too much mystery for a summer morning." Jim felt cornered, not wanting any surprises, no sudden out-of-the-blue anything.

"Gosh, sorry. It's just Sarah said—never mind. Just a casual thing. No biggie. There's a vineyard for sale. It hasn't been doing very well and we thought it would be fun to turn it around. Bill thought we should ask if you and Sarah wanted in."

"A drunk owning a vineyard. Interesting press release that, don't you think?"

"It's a financial knot, a logistical shit storm that you're the perfect guy to unravel. The books are a mess, it's heavily leveraged in all the wrong ways, the supply chain is in jeopardy all the time—Mother Nature fucking with you at every turn. It'd be like running a banana republic. Generalissimo Jim Wicklow. You'd love it."

"Here? On the Cape?"

"You can grow wine anywhere there're hot days and cool nights. Season's short, but that makes it all the more challenging. And it would be part of the whole local, sustainable thing that's happening. We'd feature the wine at the restaurant, maybe swap grapes with some of our partners in Australia."

"People swap grapes?"

"Whatever. I actually don't know that much about it. And don't want to learn, frankly. But it would be a good project for you." Jim's sympathy radar went off.

"Is this some kind of pity investment you're throwing my way? Is she in on this? What, is everyone worried about ole Jim not being in the game, worried he's barely hanging on, may go off the deep end at any moment? What a fucking bait and switch, man. Show me the view, make me feel all warm and fuzzy, and then give me some bullshit pity project to keep me busy, get me feeling like my old self again, all while you're watching like nurses on a hospital ward. I'm fine, I'm fucking fine. I don't need you to give me crumbs to play with. I'm doing fucking fine." Jim was screaming over the raging surf by the time he finished.

Mark backed away from him, raising his hands in front of his chest in surrender and apology. "I'm sorry, I'm really sorry, Jim. It's come out all wrong. I said it wrong. We went about this very badly." Jim felt he was being handled and he didn't want to look at his friend or at the screen door where he knew Sarah and Bill were now standing, watching.

Jim walked the length of the deck quickly and took the three steps down to the beach, hoping to storm off with some grace.

As soon as he hit the sand, he realized his mistake and stumbled awkwardly, moving as if he was wearing weighted moon boots. He wouldn't turn back, he was too angry, and he kept plodding through the loose sand until he got to the harder packed, damper sand near the advancing surf. He walked, not looking back, trying to cool down, trying to figure out what he was so pissed about, and how the morning had gone from bliss to this in less than ten minutes.

After Jim slipped off his Top-siders and rolled up his jeans, he felt more like he belonged on the beach. He threw off his rage in exchange for embarrassment and confusion. He found a place to sit where people wouldn't trample him. He found rest, but he couldn't find peace. All at once—although they were always humming in his background—the falling towers were with him. The whole day—the roaring jolt; the noisy chaos; hurrying with his employees down the endless stairway in the dark; the firemen coming up past them in the opposite direction; thinking, momentarily, as he hit the street that his brother Ryan wasn't there; running with tremendous speed up Greenwich Street; standing covered in white-ish dust in Cath's foyer telling her he was pretty sure their brother was dead. He lost sense of the fact that he was sitting on a beach in Cape Cod in the late summer of 2008. His facial muscles twitched as he tried not to let tears fall because at moments like this, Jim knew, the tears did not stop until he was spent and sleeping.

Sweet Ryan, who couldn't add a column of numbers right if he used Excel. Sweet Ryan, who Jim had called Stupid Ryan all through childhood. Ryan, who was good with people, looked them in the eye, touched them on the shoulder, made Jim seem human just by standing nearby and offering up a family resemblance to whoever Jim had pissed off. Ryan, who had lost his way after Black Monday in '87 and ended up building furniture in an empty garage. Ryan, who had a daughter with an ER nurse he fell in love with when he hammered a nail through his hand. Ryan, who Jim had lured back to the world to be his people person at the firm, because things were different this time. Sweet Ryan who almost drowned on a family trip to Jones Beach in 1966, a beach so much wider than the beach Jim sat on now.

This was how he felt when it all came back, when it splashed up along his internal walls like a suddenly disturbed body of water. This was hollowness, this was alone-ness, this was loss. This was what had paralyzed him and sent him north to hide out on the Cape. Jim didn't breathe or live any better up here, he just failed at simple things in private instead of in the public space of New York.

He must have nodded off, his head resting on his arms, because he only slowly became aware that his wife was sitting beside him.

"It's time for lunch, babe." Sarah said this in her usual way when he had his moments, never asking directly but leaving the door open if he wanted to tell her something.

"I'm an asshole," he said.

"Not all the time. You're just in trouble."

"I'm fine."

"Obviously."

"I'm just an asshole."

"An asshole with a body count haunting him." Jim heard Sarah's father in these words. A man he'd met only twice, a man whose worldview and vocabulary had stopped evolving sometime during his bombing missions over Vietnam.

"No Air Force brat tough-guy talk. Please."

"You don't think I know how to talk about this, that I don't know how to live through moments like this. I have an inner life, I've been to a shrink. I have words for this."

"I know." It seemed like something to say that might make her stop talking. He was the one who didn't have words for this.

"It's embarrassing that I have to explain to you that I'm not just some awesome piece of ass you got lucky with."

Jim laughed. "Fuck, can I just have a hard time every once in a while and not have to share every inner thought and turn myself into a professional head case."

"You are a professional head case. You're in trouble, babe. You have to speak. I give you room to move—because we're married. I will not give you room to go down with the ship—because we're married."

Jim looked away from her—his wife who he loved and who was right—and stared hard down the length of the beach. He would not cry. He would not swallow hard, fighting it back. He would just hold his breath until it was gone.

"I know the anniversary was hard, that it's always hard." These were the exact words he couldn't bear to hear. "It's a hard day, whether you remember or forget."

He muttered, only half-audible into the wind: "I wish."

Sarah leaned into him. Jim remained turned away from her, composing himself, putting the fragments back in their wobbly places, re-building himself blindly without a repair manual.

They returned to the house, hand in hand, walking slowly but easily in the sand. Jim gave long meaningful hugs to both Mark and Bill, hugs that began solemnly and then ended with slaps on the back and sheepish, peace-restoring grins.

At lunch, Jim and Mark talked about the vineyard and which of the beachfront houses was likely available for the right offer. Sarah tasted most of the menu and several of the wines and followed Bill through the bright yellow rooms to spy on other lunch-time patrons. She would do some thinking before issuing a verdict. On the way back to the house, weaving through the tourist throngs, Sarah put her wine-scented mouth to Jim's and moved her arm around his waist, slipping her hand into the back pocket of his jeans. Afternoon naps were announced and Jim and Sarah closed the door to the bedroom where their luggage sat unopened on the white wood floors. As they fell onto the bed, Jim licked the alcohol from his wife's tongue and listened to the ocean racing up the beach towards them.

At 3:14 a.m.—after lovemaking and an afternoon walk and dinner and a movie on DVD and deep sleep—Jim woke suddenly and with instant clarity. Sarah handed him her cell phone and he put it to his ear as he swung himself up into a sitting position on the side of the bed.

"Jimmy?" It was his sister, Cath. Her voice was thin and distant.

"Who?" He said the word, formed the question, with swollen worry. This was what he had felt coming.

"Nina." Ryan's daughter with the ER nurse. Sweet Ryan's Nina.

"I thought she was home from Iraq." In his mind there was only one place people died these days.

"She is home."

Jim thought through this meaning for a few moments.

"Jimmy. You need to come here, come down to the city. And then you need to go find her."

"Find her?" He thought, with muddled relief, phone calls like this were supposed to be about death.

"She's missing. You need to find her. You need to do this."

Jim felt himself moving, going down steps in the dark.

# FIVE

When Lise pulled into the dark canyon street, she realized Nik's place was going to be packed with people. Cars lined both sides, filled the slanted driveways of neighbors and the small patches of ground in front of the houses. This was the company she wanted. This was why she had left Danny to dinner on his own. She parked a few blocks away, below the house, and hiked up the incline. The air was dry and too hot for this time of night. She'd heard people in Los Angeles talk about fire season the last few weeks and she'd felt the Santa Ana winds in her sinuses in the afternoons. She'd been waking with a dried out head and balance problems, all of which she had put under the heading of her Iraq hangover, but maybe it was California weather instead.

There were fires in the hills somewhere north of where she was, but they seemed remote, safely encapsulated within TV coverage. All day—visiting Nina's few friends, checking the bars and restaurants Nina knew—Lise had noticed a sooty haze in the air, but this was Los Angeles, or at least close to it. She'd heard it always smelled like it was on fire. Lise flicked her tongue in her mouth. All day it had been hard to keep her lips moist.

The woods swallowed Lise as she walked away from the street. It was inky dark and then, without warning, light as she walked over the hilly terrain. Nik's house was lit up inside and there were tiki torches stuck around the outside. She saw silhouettes of the mournful drinking postures of the tribe before she could recognize faces. This was one of the rituals that gave her comfort and she embraced it, taking the first beer offered, fielding comradely hugs and searching looks.

Every gathering at Nik's felt like a wake and if you mentioned it, someone always said that someone had died or was dying. Or was lost or missing. And then Nik would get all mystical and wax on about maybe they were all already dead and they were waking themselves, the dead celebrating the dead because there was no one left alive to do it for them.

It was this kind of existential war veteran shit that Danny would eat up if he ever heard it, but made Lise reach for another beer. Along with Danny's insistence on detail—*what's that called, how do you spell it, what happened next?*—he also expected her to deliver wartime wisdom, long-winded philosophies of what war did to people so he could write Yoda-like dialogue that attracted big name actors. He had begged repeatedly to meet Nik, literally dropping to his knees as if proposing marriage. Lise would do anything to keep them apart, at least until she decided who she believed in more.

Lise walked through the clumps of men on the lawn. They saw or sensed her coming and silently parted, drifting into new geometry to let her pass. She stood too close to a tiki torch and bathed herself in the scorching air. She sipped from a cold beer can. Intrusive fragments from the past invaded. It was difficult for her to stay present. She heard Major Beck issue orders in his gently suggestive way, calming the doctors and nurses, slowing them. He prioritized life over limb. He asked for suggestions when it was clear there were no options, called times of death on occasion and more often called for an amputation set.

The traumatic amputations were surreal, like those paintings of melted clocks. Guys coming in with a limb blown off by an IED. Legs gone, an arm shredded. What was left of the men looked excessively light—as if you could just pick up their torsos and toss them onto a pile—even though the lost limb only made up a small percentage of total body weight. The loss of a leg—or two—seemed to remove the soldiers' full personhood. They were reduced to diminished parts that were no longer greater than the whole, without names or personalities or the ability to withstand a strong wind—until they looked at her with wet eyes and said with empty voices, "But I can still feel it."

Lise focused on a full set of sinewy male arms standing in the halo of one torch's brightness. He had sleeve tattoos with curly swoops and strokes of pink and green that disappeared up into the short sleeves of a T-shirt. Each time he lifted a bottle to his lips, one bicep gently swelled just enough for Lise to be reminded of her Intro to Anatomy class in nursing school. The rest of his body was lean on purpose, not from neglect. She imagined the little caverns that formed below his hipbones and disappeared down his jeans. She was sure he had an outie in the mesa of his abdomen. This was not Danny. Corporal Fantasy turned to face in another direction and she saw the caved-in skull, the patches of hair-loss, the never-healing head injury. A torch at the edge of the property suddenly fizzled out. Almost everyone jerked then settled.

A guy Lise thought of as Kansas offered her a cigarette. She thought she'd shaken him off, but he kept holding up the cigarette for her, repeatedly offering it to her with some tic he couldn't suppress, like she hadn't declined twice already. He jabbered, wired on something other than beer and nicotine.

"It's all Route Irish, everywhere you look. Secret shit is everywhere that'll blow you sky high, shred you to pieces," he sputtered and spewed.

Lise recalled the language of Iraq immediately—the abbreviations, nicknames and military-speak. Kansas was referring to the five-mile road between the airport and the Green Zone called IED Alley or Route Irish.

"They stash the shit under your car, in your fridge, it's in the water. You sure you don't want the smoke? You look like you could use it."

Lise pivoted and moved toward another bundle of men on the lawn.

Lise felt like the oldest person there. She also had all her arms and legs. She felt separate from the others. *Hold CPR check for a pulse please.* What we do to the human body. The damage we do to each other. *Anyone have suggestions? No sir.* Human beings ignited their bodies like weapons so flying metal would destroy the bodies of other human beings. *Let's call this record the date and time please.*

Lise took another beer from someone and gulped half of it. Something was in retreat and she felt spared. She knew Nik waited for her in his room, sitting in his throne-like armchair, ready to listen, to preach, to heal. But now that Lise could navigate, she wanted to try for a while longer to see if she could feel pain on her own.

She moved slowly back through the outside crowd, doing figure eights around the clusters of boys and men, and then, once inside the house, took her time, taking another beer from Maxwell, letting Acevedo cop a feel with the arm he had left. As his extant hand swept the side of her breast she felt neither fear nor desire.

She spent time in the bathroom, sitting on top of the closed toilet seat, sipping another beer and staring at the empty shower rod where her jeans had hung to dry. No one knocked needing the toilet. They were all likely peeing in the bushes or where they stood on the lawn. She washed her hands slowly, rinsed out the empty beer bottle in the sink and set it next to a tube of toothpaste. She looked in the mirror, nothing showed on her face. She was ready for Nik.

"She still gone? Still not picking up messages?" Nik's tone contained mild concern and there was also real worry held in reserve.

Lise shook her head. "I have her phone. And she's not picking up messages remotely—there are still seven unheard."

"Do you think she's with that sniper?"

Lise had been looking at the floor, unable to meet Nik's eyes in case she got pulled in too far. Now, she jerked her gaze to him, hardened her stare, keeping herself closed off. "He's a sniper?" This alarmed Lise in ways she couldn't define.

"Seriously long-range shit, apparently."

Lise had nothing to say to this.

"She's the one who's armed, is that right?" Nik asked.

Lise narrowed her eyes at Nik. "She doesn't have the gun anymore."

Nik shrugged. "That backpack she stashed here did feel a little lighter than it had been. Not that she couldn't slip an asshole a couple of Jacksons and get something else anytime."

"It's just—" Lise stopped herself from the confessional moments she felt coming, but then couldn't stop the forward progress of worry and panic. "Every day you hear about someone failing to hang on. I am barely and I…The blogs and the real-world grapevine, and every asshole screenwriter—"

"—Who you're with."

"Who I'm with. All of them with a fucking laptop and a byline going on about non-hostile weapons discharge which is so not non-hostile and there's a word for it and they won't say it and this is more than I've said out loud—or even to myself—in any way at all in months and months and months. Fuck." She clamped her lips together and vowed not to speak until spoken to.

"It's okay to cry," Nik said, trying not to make it sound as if he'd said it a thousand times before. He settled into the cushions on his chair. "It really is okay to cry, Sheridan."

She parted her lips. "I know. I will." She wouldn't, she absolutely wouldn't.

"The tough-guy act only gets you so far. You need to let go." He ran his hands through his longish and graying shag haircut. Buddha beads were wrapped four or five times around his left wrist where a watch would be on another man. A leather thong hung around his neck and disappeared down behind his T-shirt. Lise wondered what charm he wore there. She thought about it, whatever it was, lying against the skin of his chest.

"You having intrusive thoughts? Flashbacks? Stuck in a moment you can't get out of?"

Lise rolled her eyes to the ceiling. "Please. Nik."

Nik launched himself off the armchair and knelt before her on the floor. Lise froze, surprised, not sure whether to flee or fight. He placed his hands on his own thighs.

"Breathe, Sheridan. There's no emergency here. Breathe."

Lise hoped Nik wouldn't touch her. She didn't want anyone to touch her who knew what it meant to be touched. If the sleeve-tattooed hard body had merely grazed her, she would have become a million granules of sand. She wanted Danny, someone who hadn't a clue, to touch her, slip inside all her places. Danny didn't know what it meant. Nik knew and she was sure she would dissolve into the air if he put his hands on her.

"You need to let it go. You need to let yourself go. You'll end up where Nina's gone to, if you don't."

Lise met his eyes and her body vibrated a little and kept on vibrating.

"Name the fear when it comes. Recognize it, feel it and say it's okay to feel it. The problems come when you don't know you're afraid and you do things because of the fear you don't feel."

She could almost follow his thread. Phrases stuck for a moment and then fractured into nonsense.

"Maybe you should be doing some loving instead of fucking?" The words shocked Lise and she couldn't think of what or who he meant. "Do you know how to?"

Nik sprang back away from her and sat again in his chair, sinking slowly into the cushions as he landed. And as the distance between the two of them increased, Lise felt something hard being drawn out of her as if he was extracting it inch by inch and taking it on himself. She knew this was when other people would cry, but she simply sat very straight, making eye contact with him. She watched his face change. He had that look wounded soldiers sometimes got in the Cash when they were remembering what had happened to them in the field, what they had lost. It was a faraway look that told you a man was looking inside himself.

Lise looked down to the edge of the rug where it met the wood floor.

"Let us pray," Nik said.

Was he serious? Lise looked up to find Nik with his head bowed.

"We did everything we could to save Nina Wicklow, to save her life. Her friends worked hard, she worked hard to save herself. We pray that her life and her death will speed up the cause of peace or at least make those who think of war to think twice."

Lise bowed her head as well, Nik's charisma overpowering her belief in how stupid this was. Nina wasn't dead.

"We pray that Nina's life and death will end this horrible war, the violence over there and here at home. We pray that she be one of the last to suffer this way. We pray for comfort and peace and we pray for no more of this violence between men and within men—and women."

Lise thought she should smile at his addendum, but he was muttering now and she wasn't quite sure she heard the words correctly. Or maybe she was just scrambling her word salad again. And besides, Nina wasn't dead.

"We are thankful for Nina's life and we pray for all the other lives that have known what she knew. Peace not war, brothers and sisters. Truth."

Nik came to an abrupt stop and a somewhat secular end and left the room, leaving Lise to fall asleep where she was sitting.

She slept for almost forty-five minutes, the party noise beyond the door to the bedroom lulling her deeper. Lise's dream film looped between red zone and green zone. Palm trees swayed to the left in Iraq and then arced back to the right in Los Angeles. She woke, panting and alert. She tensed and listened. The noise of men drinking comforted her and she calmed instantly, feeling a familiar sense of command. She peered through the window into the dark woods. Something was out there, something in the dry night wind. Nina was out there.

Lise guided the Jetta through the three a.m. world with the
windows open, heat blowing across her body. She skirted the hills
back toward Studio City. She stopped at a red light and stared at a
glowing green sign for the Burbank Airport. One of the two cell
phones vibrated in the passenger seat. She hoped it was Nina's, but
reluctantly answered her own.

The Sierra Madre detective announced himself, but did not
apologize for the hour. Nina's uncle—her dad's brother—was flying
in to look for her. Probably the day after tomorrow. Did Lise want
to meet him when he arrived at Burbank?

"The Army's sending someone too. We'll leave from the station here and go meet his flight."

"I'll be there. What's the uncle's name?" She could hear the
detective moving papers.

"Jim something."

"Wicklow. Jim Wicklow," said Lise. Like Nina, you moron.

Lise let the light change twice, then drove on, making the turn
toward Danny's. As she pulled into the guest spot in his parking garage, she found herself spent but not sleepy. It was difficult for her
to pull the key from the ignition.

When Danny opened his door to her, she could see he no
longer thought the hours she kept strange. In that moment, in the
doorway, she saw herself as he saw her: hard and gone. What must
it be like to want to be with her—a thirty-year-old woman who rare-
ly slept at night, could drink him under the table and turned her
face away when he entered her. Lise moved her hand over his face
to shield his sleepy eyes from the bright lights of the hallway. She
vowed to try harder to be unlike herself with him, but she knew it
wouldn't hold. It wasn't holding now. She moved into the apartment, closing the door behind her, leaving them in darkness.

Danny clearly wanted to take this moment to ask about all the
things he needed to know for the screenplay and for himself. She
watched him open and close his mouth without saying anything. His
face revealed thoughts he ultimately decided not to speak of in the
murky dark of the unlit room.

"Why am I here?" She thought it was something someone else would ask.

"There's a story," Danny quietly began.

Lise sat on the edge of the coffee table and looked up at him. He was taller and older than her and looked wearier than she had ever remembered seeing him in the few elongated weeks she had known him, weeks that seemed more deeply experienced than made sense.

Danny told a story, quietly and slowly, standing over her. A story about a younger actor consulting an older actor on how to play a scene, which ended with the answer to Lise's own question: there's only one reason a woman comes to a man's home in the middle of the night.

They fell asleep together. Lise could sense the sun rising somewhere, a nearby dawn giving her the ease to sleep. She didn't dream, the unbearable stuff temporarily caroming away from her, not finding an angle in perhaps because Danny lay so close.

In the morning she used his shampoo as she showered and borrowed a cowboy shirt with pearl button-snaps he said was too small.

# SIX

Jim stood outside Cath's apartment knowing he didn't have to knock on the door. He could hear her too-high heels moving expertly and swiftly across the wood floors toward him. She was tiny, and always seemed to be exerting a strange force—one that said, you must act for me because I am too small to do it myself. Of course he had resented this constant pull—he had other things to do. He was her older brother and she knew—insisted—it meant something. Cath opened the door to him, face white under her perfect make-up, body somehow collapsed even as she stood erect on three-inch heels.

She wrapped her arms around his body, as she had not done on September 11th. He had stood then in the same spot and, whether the dusty debris had put her off or she was just so angry with him for leaving Ryan behind, she had not reached to touch him. Today, she buried a cheek in his abdomen and grabbed fistfuls of his jacket. Jim thought she might pull his clothes off. This grief—too soon— alarmed him.

"Who's here?"

Cath pushed herself from him and tried to make eye contact. Over her head Jim scanned the hallway that lay before him. He had been up and traveling for almost ten hours already and it was only one in the afternoon. He wanted a nap, maybe in the twins' room. Would they be here, the IVF ten-year-olds?

"The girls are at a friend's. Your daughter is here, but J.J. said he couldn't miss class." Children first, Jim thought. "Diana's here, she's—I don't know the word." Diana had clearly relented to Cath's place becoming command central for the search for Diana's daughter. Jim watched as Cath's face started to break open and then quickly close. "We're still losing Ryan. Every day and now this."

The defenses went up in Jim, but no further attack came. This wasn't about Ryan today—someone else had finally been lost.

"Craig's making sandwiches. You hungry?"

Yes, Jim would take a sandwich from his sister's husband.

When Jim saw Emily—a child-like fifteen with worry smeared across her wet face—he was able to anchor himself. He embraced her, relieved once again that she had stayed so childlike against the onslaught of bare midriffs and shaking ass. He feared for her, left alone in the wake of what he couldn't help but think of as an epic lap dance of 21st century adolescence.

"Nina's missing probably dead, Dad," Emily told him, as if he might be there for another reason.

"She's just missing, sweetie."

"Aunt Diana said she killed herself."

Jim felt his legs give way and he leaned on Emily too heavily before righting himself. He looked at her for more information, but she just offered, "I know, right?"

Cath click-clicked into the room and Jim turned to her, his thoughts a storm of anger and confusion. "What?" was all he could utter, urgent and feeble.

Cath shook her head. "She's not dead, but it's bad."

Emily sat next to her father and held his hand while Cath provided the details, standing in front of them, repeatedly smoothing her hands over her skirt.

"Nina couldn't settle after she came back. Diana says school didn't work out and she had trouble sleeping. Diana got her a job at the hospital filing things, but she didn't show up a lot. She partied." Emily met her father's gaze, indicating that she understood all this.

"Diana has family in California, outside Los Angeles. I'm not clear on the geography. Nina went a few months ago. She called and texted a lot, sounded good, Diana says. Something about the weather."

"It's sunny there, Dad."

Jim wasn't grateful for the information, but he slipped his arm around Emily anyway.

"She was hanging out with a lot of other kids who had been to Iraq. Diana says some were working in movies or television. You know—advising, technical advising on being in Iraq. Sharing their experience so they got it right in the shows."

"They don't get screen credits. Just money behind the scenes." Emily stated this flatly. Jim wondered how she knew things like this, how she knew these words in this order.

"Diana got a call from some police department last night."

Jim looked at Emily before asking Cath, "And she killed—she's dead?"

"No," Cath said, irritated with his leap of logic. "She's missing."

Jim turned to Emily who shrugged and offered, "Aunt Diana's saying she's dead so she might as well be."

Cath tried to speak and not cry at the same time. "Diana's a little ahead of herself here. You'll see."

"It's fucked up, Dad."

Yes, my darling daughter, it is most definitely fucked up. He left Cath and Emily for the solitude of the bathroom. As he closed the door, he heard Craig announce that sandwiches were ready.

Jim held the doorknob in its turned position as he opened the bedroom door as if letting it turn back would make such a racket that it would wake Diana. He stepped into the dark of the room, letting the light from the hallway fall across Diana's still legs. The blinds were drawn and it felt like the middle of the night. Diana did not move and Jim just stared at the back of her head turned on the pillow.

"Thank God she's a nurse," Cath whispered. "She had a prescription in her hands for Xanax about three seconds after the phone call. Craig and I drove out to Brooklyn to bring her here. She was like a noodle lying in the backseat." Cath stood behind Jim, talking to his back.

For Jim, Diana remained a mystery from the moment Ryan introduced her to him, to this moment twenty-two years later. She maybe came from money and yet also knew horrific neighborhoods Jim only heard about on local newscasts. She touched people's bodies, knew what ailed them, what they needed to do to feel better. She was practical and mystical, a combination that confused Jim in one person. He had no idea what powers she held for Ryan except that she was The One, which was a kind of magic that Jim understood only in very situational terms. His first wife had been The One for a decade or so and now Sarah was The One. Magic was fleeting for Jim, but he knew for sure that it had not been for Ryan.

"Do you remember their wedding? How pregnant she was?" Cath whispered again, reading his mind.

Jim found it hard to whisper and be heard, but he croaked back at her. "Why would she be so quick to say her kid is dead, killed herself? Why go there when you don't have to?"

"These days you have to go there. Especially with these kids."

"How bad can it get for a kid?"

"They don't know how to fix it. We learn that later."

"Is war that bad? This war, I mean. Drones and shock and awe and lasers or whatever."

Cath put a hand on Jim's arm, but he shook her off. "You know what war's like, Jimmy. You walked down sixty-eight flights of stairs, you ran when the south tower went, you lost people."

"That's not war."

"It is. Just every day."

This time he reached a hand back for her and she clasped it in both of hers. They watched over their sister-in-law together for a few moments, in the almost-dark, until the sounds of Emily and Craig talking in the kitchen seeped toward them.

"Jesus, I need a fucking drink."

Cath let go of Jim's hand. "Don't, please."

"What is this? What is all this?" He turned to her, but could only stare past her as he waited for the answer.

"It's what happens after. This is After."

"Well, there's way too much After going on around here."

Cath snorted a half-smile at her brother. "You are such a fucking moron."

"I'm getting a lot of that lately," he said.

BLT sandwiches offered a kind of nagging nostalgia for Jim, making him think of sitting on the stoop with Ryan and Cath, especially in winter, waiting to be called into the building because it was getting dark. Jim had moved away from them and moved fast toward a different life.

He looked down at his plate to find the sandwich gone. He must have eaten very quickly because everyone still had half of their food on their plates. Craig fussed with bowls of salad and coleslaw. Jim thought that both he and his sister had wives who knew food. He wanted to smile at this idea, but it was time to focus on the task at hand.

"So. I need to fly to LA?"

"If you wouldn't mind," Diana slurred from the doorway. She was wobbly on her feet, emptied out and three-benzos to the wind. She reminded Jim of himself when he had been drinking and would search the bathroom mirror for signs of life.

Jim sat with Diana on the couch while Cath and Craig took Emily to pick up the twins. Diana talked, Jim listened. Diana cried, Jim's throat swelled. Diana sipped from a water glass, Jim thought his heart would beat out of his chest. Diana lost her train of thought and stared while Jim felt his limbs tingle with anxiety and panic. He wanted to ask her for one of her pills, but it seemed impolite.

"She's going to be fine. I can't promise, but she's a kid—she's probably just gone to some party somewhere, a road trip maybe.

She'll turn up." Jim stared at the wall above Diana's head as he tried to reassure her with words he didn't know if he believed.

"You don't know how she's been. She was lost, scared, so jumpy all the time. She didn't sleep, terrible nightmares. She killed people. My girl put bullets in people. And there were so many men— God knows what she had to deal with." Diana was as hysterical as a tranquilized person could be. Jim could see the pulsing in her face and throat, see the uncontrolled flow of tears pouring out of her eyes as if there was a faucet somewhere no one knew how to close.

"I know she scares you because of Ryan, but you have to find her, bring her home. Bring her home. It'll be her body, but bring her home."

"She's not dead." Jim wasn't sure why he was so sure.

"Bring her back to me."

Jim didn't want to ask, but the need overwhelmed him. "Why do you think she scares me?"

Diana looked at him the way he had looked at J.J. as a child whenever he had to explain adult things to him. "She looks so much like him. Don't you realize? She moves like him, the way she raises her left hand when she gives directions, those dreamy eyes, the slight hitch in her walk. And she hates peas."

"I guess," Jim agreed weakly. He wasn't sure of any of this.

"I need a body this time. You know what I mean?"

"No, I—" And then he did know what she meant, remembered they had nothing to bury when Ryan died. An empty casket or urn seemed absurd in an already absurd circumstance. They had stood over a stone slab in the ground.

Later, on the plane, Jim remembered what Diana had said when he brought her yet another glass of water. "Every time you leave the room, I assume you're coming back. I know you're coming back."

He had waited for the wisdom that he hoped would follow, the hard-wrought phrase, the mantra to move forward.

"You don't get over this. I see it in the hospital, on the news. I won't ever get over this. My child is dead. Do you get over that? Jim? Do you?"

Diana had been urgent, almost reaching for him without actually raising her arms. Why did she suddenly see him as a man with answers?

"I don't know," had been his tired response. As he had said each word in turn, Jim had hoped by the third one he would have the answer.

Now, roaring across the country at thirty-six thousand feet above all the loss and mourning, Jim wished he'd reached into Diana's purse, stolen a few of her pills, just so he could keep things at bay, just so he could continue to say with great assurance that what clung to him would soon evaporate into the ether.

# SIERRA MADRE

## SEVEN

The sign that welcomed Jim to Burbank Airport buoyed him briefly before he remembered he was on an errand of potential grief and the familiar weight anchored him back into seriousness. He recalled Johnny Carson making seven or eight hundred jokes about Burbank in the years Jim had watched him, the TV illuminating the bed covers as he drifted into chuckling sleep. As he walked, Jim changed the grip on his overnight bag and peered down the long corridor of the terminal. He knew he was being met by someone.

He passed television screens that offered bits of news he felt drawn to, but he kept moving past. Sounds blared, seemed muted for a moment, then returned to normal volume. People walked toward and alongside him, making him think of currents of fish. He thought of the plips on the pond and vowed to call Sarah in the next few hours, if only to say he had landed. He hadn't turned on his cell phone, in New York or here. He liked being untethered from her.

The security area that out-going passengers struggled through was just ahead and he veered to the right to where he could exit. As he cleared the barrier he saw his welcoming committee standing off to the side, taking only a mild interest in the on-coming stream. Two of them—an older black man in a uniform and a young white woman in jeans and a buttoned-down cowboy shirt stood very straight. With them was a vaguely Hispanic man in an ill-fitting jacket and Dockers. Jim could see a police badge and part of a leather holster at his waist.

"I'm Jim Wicklow. Are you here for me?"

Introductions were exchanged among the Army representative—who turned out to be from the VA—the Sierra Madre detective, Nina's friend and Jim. The only name Jim retained was the woman's: Lise Sheridan.

To Jim, Lise looked like one of those pretty but tough prep school girls who played field hockey that he would catch sight of when he was a kid. They were always getting on and off buses. Everything about them was clean—their hair, their faces, their hands. Lise's baby-teen fat was long-gone though and she had those long lean limbs Sarah often said you got from yoga. Jim did not think Lise Sheridan had ever done yoga, but something else—something torturous—had shaped her, he could see. The skin on her face gave off no moisture or color—it was solid pavement stretched like a mask across her features. And her eyes were glassy, dark and shallow. She was either high, or in shock or both. Jim caught a shampoo scent as they both got into the back seat of the car. He shifted his gaze immediately to her breasts in his usual response to the florals of women's hair, but Lise seemed unaware of his gaze or even his presence. They looked out opposite windows as the detective pulled his car from the curb, making sure the Army guy could pull out directly behind them. The two-car caravan made its way to the Los Angeles Veterans Administration.

Jim hadn't been to Los Angeles before, but he felt he had. Everything looked almost familiar yet had a foreign non-Northeast quality. In every direction the entire state of California seemed laid out before him. It didn't take much elevation, a rise in the road as it crossed over another, to get a bird's eye view of the place. Highways were straight and wide, on-ramps looped accelerating cars into merging traffic, and off-ramps extracted vehicles into what Jim imagined were endless housing developments and dusty desert in-betweens. Downtown skyscrapers loomed in a clump surrounded by three-story decay, expensive green villages with high streets, and manicured suburbs of hidden estates and wealth that Jim knew well—the East

Coast versions, anyway. And then there was the extraordinary natural beauty of the mountains, coastline and desert beyond that Jim
had admired from afar. He felt them leave all this behind as they
pulled into the VA parking lot, the Sierra Madre detective flashing a
badge to the security guard as they rolled by.

The stench of Lysol and dirty water wafted heavily from the
linoleum floors as Jim followed the Army guy and the detective. Lise
trailed behind, walking slower the closer they got to their destination. Jim turned back as they went through a swinging door to hold
it open for Lise, but she was half a corridor behind at this point. A
television played quietly in a nearby office and he could just make
out the two anchorwomen's chirping voices, spinning their stories
and passing judgment with a quip and a tagline.

"You're a friend of Nina's?" He asked Lise.

Jim and Lise sat on a wood bench outside a set of metal doors.
Behind the doors people were preparing paperwork and offerings
they thought would be useful to Jim.

"We're friends. I'm just a little flipped out. This just reminds
me of—this place reminds me." Jim watched her stop talking, her
thoughts leaving her eyes. She looked away from him after she'd
been silent for a moment.

"You were in Iraq?"

She nodded, staring at the wall behind him.

"You were in combat?"

"I was a nurse. In the combat hospital. Green Zone." She
looked to him now, but he was afraid of what she would say next.
He held her gaze anyway and was relieved to hear her talk about how
she'd met Nina at some support group in a nearby town whose name
didn't stick in his head. Lise had been thinking about moving into
a room in the house Nina was living in. Jim drifted, not listening to
this story of two wounded women meeting and becoming sort of
friends. He felt as if he was at an AA meeting, impatient with the
shit of others.

He finally cut her off. "So this reminds you of the hospital? Flashback to Iraq kind of stuff?"

Lise widened her eyes at him. "There's a rehab facility here. This is just the office part."

Jim could tell she thought he was a douche. He wanted to apologize—maybe not apologize, but say something that was nicer, something Ryan would've known to say. Images skidded across his inner vision. Video of wounded soldiers, guys in hospital beds, sitting in a circle around a counselor. The offices, the folders and files, the order of name plates and military ranks—there was something else behind all this. He thought of flesh, blood on the floor, a shoebox containing a dead man's belongings.

"You've seen dead bodies then, right?"

Lise relaxed and fell into easy conversation with him as if something he said had flipped a switch. "Sure, lots. Not as many as you'd think. There weren't that many at the hospital in Denver and there aren't a lot of U.S. casualties in Iraq compared to other wars, but there are some. Lots of wounded."

"And Nina?"

"I don't follow."

"Nina saw dead bodies too?"

"I guess. I mean, after she'd killed them. Or on the side of the road. Or in her unit."

Jim found himself shocked by this. Of course, his niece was a soldier. That meant certain things he hadn't allowed himself to think until now. "What's that about the only person that matters in a war? I saw it in a movie maybe."

"The man to your left and the man to your right."

"That's it."

"She didn't talk about it, but I guess…she's disappeared before. Lost weekends, a day here or there. She'll turn up."

"How long have you known her?"

"Six weeks."

Jim heard this as a long time, but something in his brain worked against this sense of things. Wasn't six weeks too short of a time to know this much about a person, to know that they had bad habits, that they had killed people, to insist they were alive?

"My brother, her father Ryan—we never had a body. She was a kid, same age as my son. Fourteen, I think, yeah, fourteen. There was no body. A lot of people didn't have bodies to bury from that day."

"Nina's never said her dad was dead. I'm sorry, what day?"

"Nina didn't say?" Jim took some time to think about this. How could Nina not be saying every day that her dad had died on September 11th? He wanted to scream it every minute, wanted everyone to know, wanted to be the one who said it over and over. He never did, but he assumed she had. Being wrong about this worried him.

"My brother, Nina's dad, died in the towers on September 11th." He had never said "the towers" in his life.

"I'm sorry for your loss." It sounded automatic and Jim sensed she had said it this way a lot, maybe even been trained to say it exactly this way. She looked down into her hands, which were perched and curled in her lap like she had tried and failed to meditate in some Eastern way.

"Were you there?" Jim heard her question and wondered if anyone had ever asked him this before.

"I was. We were together and then we weren't."

Lise seemed to come alive in that second and a current of something Jim didn't recognize ran between them.

"I think she's okay. I think Nina's still here." Jim said this and immediately wondered why he believed this.

"Me too," Lise said.

Before they could recognize that they agreed on this, the detective came out through the swinging doors.

"They're ready for you, Mr. Wicklow."

"You coming?" Jim asked Lise, knowing she wouldn't.

"I'll wait here for you, sir."

The "sir" sounded forced in her mouth and it made him think she was lying, that she wouldn't be there when he emerged.

"We're looking for her. Working with the VA here. They're helping us locate a couple of people." The Sierra Madre detective looked through papers in his hands. "Everyone is very concerned." He might have said "sorry." Jim wasn't sure. Audio came and went as if someone was playing with the volume knob. Everyone was acting as if Nina was dead and this only made Jim surer that she was not. Bureaucrats were never right about anything.

After Ryan died Jim had been inundated with the oppressive helping of all the groups, the funds, the services, government agencies and NGOs, people in one kind of uniform or another. There was so much paperwork, so many phone calls to initiate and return, so much telling of the story. And this was just what Jim had to do for Ryan the employee. He couldn't imagine the reams of paper directed at Diana because Ryan had been a husband and a father. He remembered Cath saying Diana had bought a separate cell with a new number just to be able to keep track as well as to just simply turn it off when she had enough of the official taking note of Ryan's death.

He remembered Nina and J.J., sitting together on someone's couch somewhere that day or maybe the next. They were cousins at that awkward age where everything turned them on, hormonal surges sending them around the bend every time they heard a song or saw a movie or the air hit their body. They wanted to hug, to hold each other in comfort, but Jim could see the teen weirdness keeping them from touching. J.J. was safe at college now, probably drinking and screwing and going to class hung over. And Nina had been to war and was—where?

Jim watched that day as Cath sent Emily, then eight, to sit between J.J. and Nina like some neutralizing bridge. They could all hug each other then, find only what they needed. How did Cath know these things?

Jim followed Lise and the detective back to his car as the
Army guy evaporated, having completed his mission.

"I can let you know, if you call, how we're making progress.
And if you find anything, let us know." The detective abruptly
stopped walking and suddenly turned to him. "Don't go cowboy
if you find something. Vets don't always hang with a good crowd.
Don't want you getting into trouble."

Jim wasn't entirely sure what this all meant. He hoped he was
up to anything Nina's world could bring him.

"Is there some place I can drop you?" The detective wanted
this over. "Where's your hotel?"

Jim realized he hadn't booked a room and didn't want
to admit it.

"I'd like to go to this place, your town, where she's been living."

"Sierra Madre?" The detective seemed burdened by Jim's
company.

"That's where she was living?"

"Sure, whatever you want. Let's head back."

As they returned to the detective's car, Lise told Jim, "I can
show you Sierra Madre. My car's at the police station there. I can
drive you around."

Jim didn't want to be in the car with them right away and
walked off a few feet, adopting a pose that said he just needed a
minute, he'd been through something.

Jim turned his back on Lise and the detective and turned on
his cell phone. It took a moment to get service and he stared at the
screen waiting for the reassuring bars that told him he could now
connect with others.

Sarah picked up after the first ring. He wondered where she
was in the house.

"I'm on the deck. I brought the cordless out here in case you
called. The sun's setting on the pond."

"You having a glass of wine?"

"How are you? Is it bad?"

Jim looked back over at Lise and thought about how he should answer. He looked to the building where strangers moved file folders containing information about his niece. He wanted to think "absent", but the word didn't come to him right away. Was this more of the aphasia? Sarah talked, but he couldn't quite hear her.

"It's nothing," Jim said. "It's just paperwork and government people. Official shit, jargon. I guess I'm supposed to play detective." He wasn't sure what she had asked him, but he wanted to cover every possibility.

"I saw on the news there's a big fire. Is it near you?" Sarah seemed to want to list the catastrophes he might endure on this trip.

"I'm fine. I'm going to the town where she was staying so I can look around. I have to figure out what I'm actually supposed to be doing here."

"Army shit or California shit?"

Jim could hear her sip on her wine after she asked the question. He didn't answer.

"Who's with you?"

"This detective—I guess it's his case. And an Army nurse Nina met in some support group out here. Really fucked-up girl, kind of hard, but nice in a strange way."

"Sounds like your type."

Jim heard the light laughter in Sarah's voice and shifted his gaze to the sky. "Cath said I'd been through something, something like what they go through over there."

Sarah was quiet, letting Jim get the words out.

"I don't know, it's stupid. The AA shit is enough, it's enough. I can't have more shit wrong." He was man-crying a little, the tears filling his eyes but not overflowing, the lack of control stopping in his throat before it could bloom. He swallowed it all back down. "Look, they're waiting for me. And there's this stupid weather."

"Fire season."

Jim looked away from the sky and found some mountains to focus on. There was a black haze over them and it seemed to be swirling toward him. "Yeah, it's hot and dry and those winds."

"Santa Ana winds. Do you want me to come out there?" Her voice seemed constrained, like she was trying not to talk about something else.

"No, I don't think so. I'm okay. It's just hard to know what to do. I feel like I'm in a movie. There's a script, but it seems weird following it."

"Just ask the people who know her where she might be."

Jim immediately looked down at the pavement at his feet. "I'm going now. I'll call you later."

"Love you, babe."

"Yeah. Me too." He pulled the phone away from his face and spun around.

He could see Lise and the detective waiting in the car, careful not to look at him, the AC running. Jim stood in the dry hot air and wondered how he could make his legs move.

In Sierra Madre, Jim followed Lise out of the detective's car in the police station parking lot. She remotely popped the trunk on a dusty black Jetta and he dropped his bag into it. The Jetta was squeezed in between two police SUVs and she had to pull it out of the spot before he could get in the passenger-side door. The inside of the car was spotless and Jim worried about dirtying it or leaving marks if he touched anything. He gingerly snapped the seat belt clip into place and tried not to wonder if she was a good driver.

They only drove a few blocks before Lise slid the car into an open spot in front of a Starbucks. Jim admired how efficiently she parked the car in one smooth move. She would do okay in New York.

"I need some caffeine. You?" She asked.

Jim could also do with something to eat—it was dinnertime in the East—and he found himself craving Mexican food.

"Denver's Mexican is better, but the tacos are okay at this one place," Lise insisted. Jim was confused: shouldn't the Mexican food be amazing in California? He wanted to check with Sarah, she would know.

He felt out of place engaging in what he considered domestic activities with this woman who wasn't his wife. The Starbucks menu defeated him into the submissive order of a large coffee that was immediately corrected into a call for a *grande* drip. Lise's complicated order involved the words "red eye" and he wondered if she would get more or less tense from drinking it. They left the Starbucks with their coffees, walked two blocks and sat at a small metal table outside the Mexican restaurant that served the okay tacos. He peered through the window and saw a television above the bar, a batter taking a pitch without swinging.

The commercial center of the town looked alien to him. It was both too small and too big and was transected by streets of the wrong width. There was a small town square that was more of a triangle. Pavement sidewalks and tar roads softened in the heat. He looked up one of the streets and could see an overcrowded sort-of-suburb with houses very close together on small lots. There were private lawns between driveways and public green strips along the curbs. He could see from the angle of some of the streets that they were in the foothills of mountains. He wondered what the canyons among the hills looked like.

"You ever see *The Rockford Files*?" Jim asked and immediately regretted it. She was too young. He shoved part of a soft taco in his mouth to stop himself from saying anything else.

"My dad's mentioned it, I think. Guy had a car that was cool, lived at the beach?"

Jim remembered liking the car, but he couldn't think of the make or model or color. He had thought of the show because Sierra Madre reminded him of the towns that Rockford visited whenever he left L.A. for an out-of-town case. There was something vaguely old-timey western about them even though everybody wore flared,

high-waisted polyester pants and drove Cadillacs. The towns were
portrayed as less civilized—and certainly less intelligent—than big
city Los Angeles. Rockford always seemed to be talking his way
into tight spots with a lot of smart-ass chatter and biting words. Jim
couldn't remember if Rockford even carried a gun. Someone else
was always saving him at the last minute, especially in these remote
towns. Sierra Madre felt like one of these places—remote, slightly
stupid, inhospitable to outsiders—but Jim didn't feel armed in any
way, with words or weapons, to get out of trouble.

"Can I see where Nina is living?" Jim wiped his mouth with
the paper napkin after he said this to give Lise some time to answer.

"She put everything in its place. It's very neat." Lise said. This
sounded to Jim like a warning Lise was ashamed of. He looked at the
top of her head as she bowed to look through the metal criss-cross
of the tabletop. Jim imagined a handwritten note placed on a small
kitchen table. No, he would not think these things.

"So we can go? Can we walk from here or do we need to
take the car?"

"I'm going to need to make a stop first, but, yeah, we can walk."

Jim paid the bill. The place didn't take credit cards and he used
what little cash he had.

They walked away from the last bites of their tacos, throwing
their crumpled moist napkins among the bits of salsa fresca and
tortilla stubs.

"Where do you need to stop?" Jim asked.

Lise didn't answer him.

Jim followed her into the Buccaneer Lounge, realizing only after they crossed the threshold what he had walked into. He stopped
himself slowly, bringing his feet to a halt, watching Lise continue
into the place. She walked half the length of the bar and slid onto
a stool. Jim watched as she ordered, took a sip from the beer bottle the bartender brought her, and settled into a lost drinking pose.
The television behind the bar streamed numerical hysteria, but Jim
turned from its visual noise and stared at the glistening array of bot-

tles. Deafness clogged his ears. He watched Lise realize Jim wasn't with her and turn to look for him.

Jim stared through the dim light of the bar at Lise. Neither he nor she seemed to know what to do next. Jim couldn't move from where he stood just inside the door and Lise appeared anchored to her seat. After a few moments Jim found he was able to move his feet and put one in front of the other and walked to her.

"I can't be in here. I'll wait for you outside," he heard himself say as his hearing returned.

Lise nodded and turned away from him.

As Jim retraced his steps back to the door, he realized he'd been holding his breath. He let it go and then took a deep inhale. And just as he went out the door, he filled his nasal passages with the stinging and slightly nauseating scent of liquor he couldn't drink.

# EIGHT

Lise walked along the suburban sidewalk. Jim followed a few steps behind, not really trying to catch up. As she turned the street corner, she felt herself evaporate. It was as if she suddenly existed only in her head and her presence in the present world melted away into a fumbling misapprehension of her jumbled brain. She discovered herself standing at the front door of the rental house, having walked along the sidewalk, through the gate, along the side path to the small house, all without registering any of these experiences. This blinking in and out didn't happen as often as it had when she was at Walter Reed.

She pulled the wood door and then the screen door toward her, holding them both for Jim. She stepped into the small house in full command, for the moment, of herself in the world.

She propelled herself into the living room and Jim quickly followed. Lise paused for an instant, looking for evidence, searching for something she had missed that would tell her where Nina was. "The landlady, Jen, is nice most of the time."

Jen was from New York too, Lise remembered. Maybe she knew Nina's uncle.

Jim pretended he was very interested in the fabric of the saggy couch.

"Mr. Wicklow, sir, it's okay to look around."

Jim stood up straight, looked directly at everything in the room, but Lise saw a slight tremor in his right hand.

"Do you live here too? Did you say?" Jim looked at Lise when he asked, but his eyes drifted. Lise watched him latch onto the blank canvas of the wall.

She gestured for him to sit on the couch and they sat there together staring at the brand new flat screen TV leaning against the wall already looking like discarded junk. Jen's husband hadn't gotten around to hanging it.

"Do you think we should turn it on?" Jim asked this strangely, seeking both Lise's permission and advice. Lise couldn't imagine what he might want to watch, but she guessed he needed to drown out the fact that he might not remember what Nina looked like. "I'd like to catch up on the news. I feel kind of out of touch all of a sudden."

"Were you on vacation?" Lise asked.

"I don't understand."

"The detective said you were in Cape Cod. Were you on vacation?"

"I live there now. I moved there a few years ago to get away from the city. After, you know."

Lise didn't really take this in. She hadn't really cared about the answer to her question or the logistics of Jim's life.

Time seemed optional to Lise once again. She watched their reflections in the unlit TV screen, slightly distorted but reassuring in that they confirmed their existence. She tasted beer in her mouth and immediately wished she'd taken that cigarette from Kansas the other night, if only to have saved it for this moment. She felt the caffeine working against the alcohol, keeping her up, keeping her tense. She felt anchored in place and then immediately thought of Denver.

When Lise was first discharged she went home to Denver. She had given up her apartment before she deployed and her belongings were in storage. She dropped her suitcases on the floor of her old room—now a guest room—at her parents'. She hardly slept there. She stayed with friends or went to all-night parties. Sometimes, after a one-night stand, she would sleep in her ancient Taurus parked on a quiet street. Her old job in the ER at Saint Anthony North was hers again if she wanted it and she did, but she couldn't make a decision.

No one asked her what she was doing or what she had planned. To the people at home, Lise was still gone.

Ye olde Taurus finally gave out after a billion miles, failing to start near dawn in front of a downtown loft building after several rounds of margaritas and Bill or Ben. As Lise walked to where she thought she could find a cab, she decided in an inexact way that she might want to change a few elements of her life. That afternoon, struggling to balance a hangover and her new resolve, she read an email from Major Beck. He was home in California getting ready to redeploy. The San Gabriel Valley was a nice place to live, there were lots of nursing jobs and a friend of a friend knew some movie and TV people who wanted to work with veterans, give them money for their stories. Was she interested?

"Are you here?" Apparently this was the second time Jim had asked Lise this question.

"Yes of course." She slotted back into the present with a click and a rush of information. "No, I don't live here. I have a room over someone's garage nearby. One of my commanding officers, Major Beck lives there with his family. He let me have a room. Nina and I were talking about me moving into the other bedroom. It's closer to Nik's than where I've been staying, so I was thinking about it."

"Is Nik your boyfriend?"

Lise laughed out loud making real laughing noises she couldn't remember making in a long time. "Nik runs the support group Nina and I go to. He's a Vietnam veteran. We spend a lot of time there—when he's not being a dick." She was talking about weeks, but it felt like years.

"What's he a dick about?" She could tell Jim was genuinely curious.

"He's one of those guys who's a dick about everything. Know what I'm saying?"

Jim looked away from her and Lise wondered how he could know. He wasn't a boots-on-the-ground kind of guy. More of a Mr. Money who'd gotten pissed on.

"Do you want to see Nina's room?" Lise wanted to give Jim something, remind him why he was there.

They stood in the doorway to the small bedroom. The windows were huge and the sills were close to the ground. It was nice when there was a breeze, but the air now was still and dry.

"That's her stuff." Lise pointed to the closet. She watched Jim recognize the messenger bag. "The sheets belong to the landlady. It's semi-furnished, the house."

"I guess Nina left most of her things at home in Brooklyn."

"She's just visiting," Lise said, meaning it one way when she said it, but hearing the second way.

The small house grew dark around them and a strong wind gusted, bringing thick dirty air in through the screens. Lise could smell something burning and she wondered how close the fire was, how far the wind was carrying the scent. Danny said ash filled the air when the weather got like this.

"It smells like that day a little," Jim said. "Things burning. Buildings, jet fuel, maybe even people." Lise gave her own images to these words, from Iraq and from the television news Danny had watched that morning.

Lise was thinking so deeply about the destructive power of fire that she didn't feel Jim at first, but then she awoke to the fact his hand was on the small of her back and he was facing her. She looked down at their shoes.

"Mr. Wicklow, sir?" She didn't think she needed to move and she was relieved to find herself breathing so she just stood there, staring at the floorboards, waiting for him to do or say something else. She wondered if she was feeling anything.

"I'm sorry, I was just, for a second there—I'm married, I'm sorry." He pulled his hand away and stood up straighter so they weren't standing so close. "Look, are you all set? I mean, do you need money or anything?"

It was hard to imagine this strange man was so closely related to her friend. Lise wondered what his brother had been like. How could Jim walk around like this? It was fear—other people's fear was like this: clumsy, imprecise, dense.

Lise's fear was different. In some ways it wasn't even fear. The war had taken so many things from her, from her body, from her mind and from the other part of her that hovered between actions and thoughts. She didn't want these things back—she wasn't even sure what they were—she just wanted some kind of something to reassemble her broken world.

"I already looked through her stuff. Maybe if you look—" Lise desperately wanted to get Jim moving forward.

Jim gently pawed through the clothes Nina had hung in the closet. He didn't seem to have any reactions to them. They were completely neutral pieces of fabric. Lise had expected some comment about the length, the color, the quality—maybe if he'd been a woman. He sat on the very edge of the bed and hesitated before opening the drawer of the small table.

"That's where I found her phone."

Jim pulled his hand from the empty drawer. "Can I see it?"

They looked at the phone in Lise's palm. She cracked it open to reveal the locked display.

"Any ideas on a password?" Lise looked to Jim with her version of hope.

"I'll think about it." He took the phone from her, snapped it shut and disappeared into the bathroom.

"What's all this?" Lise heard him say, thinking she was standing next to him.

When she joined him amid the clean white tiles, she saw he had the medicine cabinet open. Pill bottles filled most of the shelves along with a box of Band-Aids and a half-smoked joint.

Lise didn't have to read the labels to know what the bottles contained, but she said them aloud for Jim. Celexa, Trazodone, oxycodone, Klonopin, Xanax.

"Is that bad stuff to be on?"

Lise thought of her own collection of medicines. She wasn't sure where they were. Had she taken her morning doses or had she forgotten?

"It's standard. It's what the VA gives you."

Jim nudged the joint to the side with his thumb and picked up a flesh colored patch. "What's this?"

"Looks like a nicotine patch to me," she lied.

"Bullshit."

No one usually knew when she was lying and she couldn't figure out how she felt about this, but she would give him the truth. "It's Fentenyl. It's used for extreme pain. The army uses it in lozenge form in the field now instead of morphine. Kind of an opiate upgrade for the modern soldier."

She watched Jim slip the patch into the pocket of his jacket. "For when we find her," he said, grabbing a bottle as well.

Lise stood very close to Jim for a few moments longer, testing to see if her responses changed, if she could still breathe. Her throat gently pulsed too tightly for just an instant so she stepped away from him and back into the bedroom. This brought her less relief than she hoped.

She had an imperfect memory of the rocket attack in the Green Zone the day she hit her head. She recalled moments in the Cash, but she was on her fast feet treating soldiers so they weren't from that day—those memories were from the other days. She had better but eerier memories lying in mid-flight limbo on the way to Ramstein for observation and treatment. But those images merged with the flight to Walter Reed and the memory exercises and the scans and blood draws. Doctors were always moving their fingers along her scalp, moving through her hair like a thresher, not mixing or separating anything, just searching for external evidence of her injury. She'd smelled fire then too—no, that was wrong. She had smelled oranges, on and off for weeks. Now she smelled fire—no, it was ash that filled her nostrils. There was light twirling ash now, coming in through the window screens.

Jim stood by the wall, running his hand along the wall paint. Lise wanted to be as far away from him as possible yet she felt simultaneously compelled to stay in Nina's house with him. Why were they there? Was she waiting for him to finish whatever it was he was doing—looking for clues, maybe? Wasn't he supposed to be out somewhere searching for her? He acted as if he was paying respects.

Lise drifted to Iraq to the streets near Danny's to the bartender at the Moon to the Cash to the Saint Anthony ER to a final history exam at DU to reading *We Were The Mulvaneys* on the porch of the student house she lived in during nursing school to an awesome plate of enchiladas made with green chiles to a cold Coor's to snow falling on the back of her neck to riding a bike when she was in fifth grade to Sheryl Crow blasting from a car radio to Acevedo's long-gone arm to that smell in the corridor of her Green Zone residence which was not Lysol or oranges or blood or anything she could remember now.

She looked over at Jim. He seemed very far away from her, which was both a good thing and not. She imagined embracing him as a child would a parent with reverse comfort, but she knew she couldn't pull it off. He had charged the spaces between them with sex and she wouldn't be able to make it go away. She could hug him around the waist with her head on his chest and find a neutral instant before the charge caught. She could move her limbs and his as if their bodies were rushing toward a definitive act. She could pull open the front of her shirt, the pearl button-snaps giving way with a satisfying series of clicks. She could take Jim's head in her hands and press it against the bare skin of her chest.

She could also imagine pulling a serrated knife out of the drawer in the kitchen and pushing it across Jim's neck. But then she would have to repair him.

Later, when it seemed the house couldn't get any darker, Jim stepped toward Lise and asked if she wanted him to call someone.

"Why?" Lise was afraid she'd missed a moment again.

"Because you're crying. And I think you, ah, peed in your pants."

Lise's senses returned slowly. Her tears closed around her throat and she couldn't speak.

Jim slowly re-buttoned the pearl snaps on her shirt one by one from the bottom to the top, pausing only slightly as his hands came near her breasts. Lise couldn't remember how her shirt had come open.

"Thank you, sir." Lise managed to squeak this out through the tears that still streamed.

"Let's start over," Nina's uncle said to her. "My name is Jim. Call me Jim."

"Okay." Lise was still crying, starting to feel the damp urine in the crotch of her jeans.

"We'll find Nina. She's alive," he said. "No more stupid shit."

To Lise, Jim didn't look too sure of his promises. "We need to find her," Lise told him.

Jim stood very close to her again. She flinched.

He didn't jerk away, he simply said, "I'm going to carry you the way I would pick up my daughter when she was little. We'll get you cleaned up."

Lise didn't move or speak, she just looked at him, waiting for it to happen.

# NINE

Jen Broder lay on her bed and watched out the window as Lise and the man went into her rental house. The smell of fire was everywhere. She'd been watching the world from this position for a couple of days. She hadn't been able to leave her bedroom since mid-way through Mia's birthday party. She'd conducted some business—checking on the condo and the house on Mira Monte, monitoring credit card balances, inquiring about a two-month opening at a small ad agency in Pasadena—all from the phone at her bedside. She'd also spoken to Lise once—*still looking for her*—and Nina's mother twice from the new cell phone when it became clear that Nina was now missing and not just simply away from home—decided by someone somewhere. Jen wasn't sure how this had been determined.

She recognized the man with Lise—apparently Nina's uncle—from her New York days, thinking she'd slept with him. He worked with money, she thought, but didn't quite remember. She had the sensation that at any moment all of her past would knock on her front door. It was like one of those nightmares where you dream you go to a party and everyone you've ever had sex with is there, including the lesbian from sophomore year. It was like when she looked at the mortgage balances for her three properties or her credit card bills: a kind of out-of-control skidding away of anything that resembled a way out.

Jen lay on top of the light blanket she had placed over the sheets when she made the bed. She ran her fingers over the soft knitted ridges of the pale green coverlet. She had bought one in each color. She often bought clothing and linens in all the colors they came in. It made her feel like a collector of fine things, someone who had taste and was only satisfied with the full set. *I'll take one of each.*

She could hear Mia practicing her scales on the small upright piano in the living room. She thought about telling her to stop—*Mommy has a headache*—but the repetition was comforting, like constant pain. The little girl was likely still wearing her favorite birthday gift, a bow and quiver of arrows, plastic replicas of those worn by an animated warrior princess that was this month's obsession. Jen wasn't sure who had given the gift to Mia. Marco had gone to pick up take-out at the okay Mexican place and would be back soon. She'd have to nuke some chicken fingers and broccoli for Mia. Jen planned to have a second beer with her dinner tonight. She'd had too much coffee and neither the Ativan nor the Paxil was doing what it promised.

Diana had said during the second phone call that she would send her brother-in-law—*Ryan's brother will come get her*—to search for Nina. Jen wondered if someone stopped being an in-law if the connecting spouse died. People said "ex" when they got divorced, but this seemed different. This in-law was now in one of her rental homes and maybe she knew him from before.

Jen was beginning to feel she was at the root of Nina's disappearance. She felt responsible for Nina being in Sierra Madre. It was supposed to have been a safety line she was throwing to this distant relative, but now it felt like the beginning of a bad chain reaction. Jen knew Danny from the ad agency in New York. She bumped into him in Old Town Pasadena, in front of Il Fornaio, and he had said he and some other screenwriters wanted to talk to Iraq veterans. Jen had told Diana, which became the reason for Nina's escape from despair in New York and her new start in Sierra Madre. Jen had also told Dr. Beck, a parent at Mia's school, when he got home from Iraq,

and he had connected Danny to Lise, another damaged warrior looking for—what exactly? When Jen thought of the sequence of events
it felt like one of those TV stunts with a million dominos lined up in
some elaborate shape. It felt like things falling inevitably, endlessly.

Jen hardly knew Diana. They'd met only a few times and it
took a mass family reunion to tell them they were related. Then they
had bumped into each other in the middle of the day at a Cobble
Hill bar on the first anniversary of September 11th and had shared
secrets, stories and vodka on the rocks. Diana hadn't wanted to talk
about her husband or his death. *Can we talk about the bartender's tattoos
instead?* Jen had pumped and dumped enough breast milk for Mia
that morning to get plastered. She was going to stop breastfeeding
soon, she just didn't know when. Was that the day she had slept with
the money guy? No, he didn't seem like a Brooklyn guy.

Jen thought of Nina moving along the edges of the living
room during Mia's birthday party, shrinking away from the vibrating seven-year-olds, eating Mia's chocolate birthday cake just hours
before she—what, went missing? Nina was a troubled girl and when
troubled girls go missing, they usually end up dead. Jen herself had
been troubled, but she had always come back from the outlands.

Marco had sat on the edge of Mia's big-girl bed the night before telling her that some people—other people—are just so hurt
they are beyond anyone's reach. *Sometimes people just feel really alone.*
Mia thought more cake or another song on the piano would make
sad people hurt less, but Marco had said cake didn't work like that.
Jen had eavesdropped on the conversation between her husband
and her daughter and worried about what she was hearing. Jen had
been Nina once or a version of her.

Shit, what was the money guy's name? Mike, maybe. Jen scur-
ried through the partying corridors of her memory, but kept shutting doors and turning away at the powders lined up along glass
tables, the scary people in the shadows, the middle-of-the-night
staggering walks of shame. When she was fifteen, maybe sixteen,
running around nighttime Manhattan, going to clubs and bars, or-

dering Apricot Sours as if they didn't give away her age, she lost her virginity only half-willingly—but later decided not to count it—in a bathroom stall in the unisex restrooms at the Mudd Club to a guy who said he was a senior at Regis and who she imagined looked like John Lurie of the Lounge Lizards. She felt pursued and beaten in panicked waves for months afterward. The feeling would return not often, not all the time. It wasn't a rape. It was something close, but it wasn't rape. She thought it was more of a shock, but definitely not a rape. Like the feeling, this thought would return not often, not all the time. Years later, six months into their dating, Marco had asked Jen to stop flinching when he kissed her.

She wasn't sure what had existed between being young and then being this working adult with a job and a boyfriend, but she knew if she didn't stop with Marco—this man who liked walking slowly down the street with his arm around her—she would slip back into a place from which she would never emerge. He said Stop, and she did. She got clean while working sixty-hour weeks at the agency and finding room for Marco in her apartment among her many belongings. She was earning money in advertising, buying things—everything—and it made her feel just as complete as a line of coke and an Absolut on the rocks had. There was no drudgery in that particular bout of sobriety—that came later. She had been pleasurably clean for almost three years when she realized she was very pregnant.

She relapsed deliberately on the first anniversary in that Cobble Hill bar with Diana, vowing that she wasn't in trouble but in some newly informed and improved control.

"You need more restraint," Marco had said, standing in the kitchen late one night watching her bob and weave away from him so he wouldn't taste booze or another man in her mouth. "Will power isn't working."

"What do we do?" was all Jen could ask, not from drunkenness but from complete confusion as to what they were talking about.

She watched him open his mouth and then close it. She could see his face change with everything he thought to say and then decide not to say. She watched him look toward Mia's room and then back at her. He had been hoping, Googling, imagining another life for them.

"Let's move to California," he said.

Jen felt his words break apart the hardness inside her.

"My friend Gary needs a tech director for his new thing. You could work at an agency in Pasadena or even L.A. My folks can watch Mia."

"You've figured it out." She hadn't meant to sound accusing. She actually admired him at that moment and the way he said the word "California" made her feel something.

He had pulled her to him then, but she had jerked her head violently one way and then another as he tried to kiss her. "I don't care who it was," he had said. "Just make it me again."

They had desired each other in New York and now they felt the opposite of that. They had moved to Sierra Madre, near Marco's boyhood home, where they hoped they could get back to—what? Their interests shifted. They had bought houses and a condo with little money down, the same with cars and clothes and things for Mia and for the house, and they had taken trips and stayed at resorts, and Marco had bought himself a Triumph—all with money they earned and then with credit they had seemingly earned as well.

Now Jen lay on her bed trying to remember the name of a man who worked with money that she wasn't even sure she'd had sex with.

"Mommy?" Mia stood in the doorway, the braided ropes of the quiver visible at her shoulders. "I'm hungry. Is dinner late?"

"I'm sorry, Bean, we're having dinner at grown-up time tonight."

Mia stood at a distance, weighing her options. Jen could see her assessing her mother's mood and her own. Was she afraid of this woman who had been in bed for three days or did she miss her AWOL mom terribly and want loving attention. Mia came to a decision and suddenly bounded onto the bed, plastic arrows rattling, rocking Jen around on the soft mattress. She lay facing her mother, mirroring her pose, one arm dramatically displayed across a pillow.

"Would you like dessert before dinner?"

Mia's eyes went wide in a comic take. "Joe-Joe's?"

Jen nodded.

Mia fled the room and returned instantly with a cellophane roll of Trader Joe's version of Oreos. Jen wondered if her daughter had mastered astral projection during a visit to Marco's father at Cal Tech.

"Hey Bean, when you went to went to visit Grandpa Leo at his lab—did he do an experiment with you or anything?"

"Just once," Mia answered, with a grown-up smile. "Can you do this for me, please?" Mia held out the roll of cookies. Her hands had not caught up with the rest of her and she had a hard time using her fingers in precise ways. Her piano playing was the least effected.

Jen opened with: "Just two before dinner, okay?"

Mia countered: "Four, I think."

Jen stood firm: "Two or none."

Mia raised: "I have to eat one for Nina since she's not here."

Jen folded: "Three and no more."

Jen split the plastic and the cookies rolled onto the blanket.

"Uh oh," Mia said. "Crumbs in the sheets." She looked at her mother, fearing anger but instead found Jen offering a conspiratorial eyebrow raise.

"We don't have to tell Daddy, right?" Jen whispered. "Unless he rolls over onto a Joe-Joe in his sleep, then we'll have to," she teased. She grabbed her daughter and mutual tickling ensued with ringing peals of laughter and smothering hugs. Jen held her breath as she held her daughter just in case this might all disappear.

How had she survived all the things she had tried? How had she lived to the exhausting age of forty-six? Why wasn't she dead in a street accident or living in some shit hole addicted to some harrowing drug or dying of AIDS in some publicly funded hospice or standing humiliated in bankruptcy court wearing her last pair of designer jeans or pouring a really fat version of herself into a blazer for client meetings at some totally un-cool agency back in New York. *Hey lady, you can't sleep here.* Jen looked at Mia crunching away with great seriousness on a cookie, almost-black crumbs staining her lips, and she wondered just how much she was going to screw up her kid. Maybe she'd done it already. *Ma'am, I'm sorry to tell you, but your child has*—Something she'd ingested somewhere along the line had altered her and she had passed it on to Mia, a ticking clock waiting to run down.

Was the money guy named Sean? That didn't seem right.

"Dinner!" Marco called from the kitchen. She hadn't heard the car in the driveway or him entering the house.

"Daddy." Mia fled the bedroom again.

Jen knew she had to get up off the bed, knew she had to leave this room that she had been in for days. Marco was sick of accommodating her downward slide, bringing her food and beverages, making excuses with friends and Mia. She knew he hadn't taken down the party decorations, leaving them hanging, urging her to do it. They had been extreme-fighting in angry whispered tones—*how could you spend money on that?*—for over a year now so the demands of the last three days hardly seemed like something new between them, but she knew they were nearing some kind of dead end. When someone goes missing this close to home Jen knew there would be consequences.

"Mommy! Dinner!" Mia screeched from half a house away.

Jen got off the bed and felt the fluids in her brain find their new levels. She exchanged her sneakers for flip flops. She pulled to her nose the two brightly colored T-shirts she had layered on herself. They didn't smell fresh, but they didn't smell like she'd been wearing them for three days either. She left the top button undone on her jeans and even pulled the zipper down a notch. The beers would expand her stomach. She pulled the shirts over her un-buttoned waist.

Jen walked into the kitchen feeling as if she had just recovered from a fever. Everything seemed oddly and exceptionally clean. Mia sat erect in a chair at the kitchen table waiting with a fork and knife, one in each fist. Marco seemed tall and warm as he pulled Mexican food from white paper bags. In their New York kitchen, when he would reach for something on the highest shelf, his soft, overwashed T-shirts would rise to reveal the dark trail of hair along his stomach. Jen would stop what she was doing, bend down and blow a raspberry on his incredibly ticklish stomach. He would swallow a shriek, shrinking away from her as she vibrated her sloppy wet lips. She had thought these were the most astonishing moments in their life together—her mouth on his flesh, him suppressing laughter, their joy.

Now, Jen slid her arm around her lanky, low-waisted man as she joined him at the counter. She could see that he had not ordered the carnitas tacos she had asked for. He leaned into her, remembered it was her and quickly moved away to place things on the table. Except for a hurried hate-fuck in the middle of an epic screaming battle over how much money they owed, they had not touched each other all summer.

Jen placed chicken fingers on a plate in the microwave and then chopped broccoli. Marco laid out the tacos and hot sauce, guacamole and chips on the table. Mia sat poised, ready to pounce on her food as soon as it was placed in front of her. Her parents moved around her, satellites orbiting a young planet.

Mia dropped her chin to her chest as Jen placed her plate in front of her. The little girl muttered something to herself as Jen watched with great curiosity.

"What are you doing?" Jen asked.

"Saying grace, thanking God for my food," Mia answered flatly and plunged her fork into a chicken finger.

Jen looked to Marco who busied himself with his tacos, indicating he was sitting this one out. *I'll teach her C++ and how to throw a baseball.*

"Where'd you learn that?" Jen asked.

Mia chewed thoughtfully and swallowed before answering.

"Miss Janet says grace before she eats lunch at school. I also said a prayer for all the people I know in heaven. Is that okay?" Mia didn't seem to care about the answer as she attacked her broccoli.

"Of course," Jen said, although she wasn't sure. Jen couldn't remember her tribe's—or, more accurately, her grandmother's—position on heaven and hell. "Who do you know in heaven?"

"Grandpa Rich, Martin Luther King and maybe Nina."

Jen was chilled by the quick and all-encompassing answer: Jen's father, an historical figure, and their missing tenant. This slightly insane and yet very logical small person had been inside Jen's belly and now sat chomping on dinner while listing her celestial acquaintances. These kinds of events were always happening though. Every school day seemed to transform the child. There was always some surprising revelation, something she had learned, something she now believed absolutely.

On September 11, 2001, Jen's water broke while she walked home from the Brooklyn Promenade after watching the altered skyline across the water reveal itself. Papers, whole and shredded, floated in the air around her as she walked home, stopping once to lean against a building as labor pains flooded her. Meanwhile, Marco was riding on the back of a friend's motorcycle plowing through a swung-open car door and the streaming fleeing crowds, accelerating across the Brooklyn Bridge toward home. *Go go go go go!* Mia wanted into this broken world and even then her parents were apart and unprepared, battling the elements. Twenty-six hours later Mia emerged, an old soul.

Jen sat down, joining her daughter and husband at the table. Marco took a long pull from a bottle of Pacifico. He had not gotten one for her.

He spoke without looking at her. "You see what's happening on the news?"

"Is it another?" Jen still didn't have code words for that day.

"No, not that kind of thing." Marco shot a look at her and then at Mia and then back to his food. "Wall Street's in meltdown. The economy's disappearing or something."

"Tech glitch?"

Marco pursed his lips and shook his head. Jen couldn't tell if he was overwhelmed by the seriousness of what he said was happening or if he was just pissed that she had immediately thought to blame the techies.

Jen watched Marco and Mia eat for a few moments, trying to figure out if she was going to rise from her chair. Eventually, she did get up and search through the fridge for another beer. There was so much food in there, some freshly bought, some rotting, some that would survive another disaster. Did mustard ever go bad? She found two Pacificos, placed them near her plate, claiming them both for herself.

The first sip was extraordinary in how quickly it revived her. She wanted to conjure an honorary salute for Nina, but she couldn't think of what it should be. Jen slid a hand under the table and found Marco's denim thigh, not to start something, just to connect. His angry look softened and he shifted his gaze from the guacamole to her. Jim, that was his name. Jim the money guy.

# TEN

Lise let Jim lift her off the ground. Whatever currents ran between them had reverted to a comradely sense of common cause. As he carried her, she hung herself over his shoulder and looked at the back of his shirt collar as it disappeared under his hair, which she thought kind of long for an East Coast money man. But she guessed he was maybe not that man anymore. If there was a chaste way to undress a woman, comfort her without coming onto her, he had found it. The occasional waft of piss in the air had added a trace of medicinal ministrations, as if they were in a hospital. These were not the elements of tender care Lise was used to, but she gave herself up to them and to him, as she would have to the liquor and the music.

Jim placed her on the closed toilet seat. He turned away to run the bath water and she immediately removed her clothes. She sat there naked while he busied himself testing water temperature and then reading the instructions on the bottle of bath gel. Lise watched him squeeze the gel into the water and she smelled lemons. She saw the foamy bubbles form on the top of the water and as Jim bent to gather up her clothes, Lise stepped behind him and into the tub and under cover of the white foam.

"Who should I call?" Jim asked.

She told him.

Lise lay in the cooling bath water of Nina's tub. The bubbles from the citrusy gel Jim had poured in had dissolved long ago. She felt safer when the water was hot and she lay under the lemony foam head. Now, she was starting to feel exposed, in danger.

Danny sat on the floor with his back to the tub. He was very angry. He had gotten a call from some guy he didn't know, some guy who told him Lise needed him. And when Danny had arrived—as knight-like as he could manage after seventy minutes in LA County traffic in his Honda Civic Hybrid—he found a strange man standing guard over his naked woman who was taking a bubble bath and didn't seem like she was struggling with her shit at all.

"Can you wear Nina's clothes?" Danny didn't look at her.

"I'll grab another pair of her jeans. Your shirt's okay. My sneakers are kind of shot, they'll take forever to dry."

"Not that they didn't stink before," he said, finally turning to her with a small smile, ready to show he was going to be angry only a little while longer. "Ever heard of socks, lady?"

Lise could handle this kind of conversation with him. "It's LA, man. Don't need no stinking socks."

"Stinking is right," he said as he rose from the tiles. "You'll be okay for a minute? I want to see what New York Man is up to."

A few moments later Lise could hear the two men talking on the other side of the door. It sounded like surgeons mumbling over a body.

She wrapped one towel around her waist and another under her arms. She felt armored as she opened the door and moved to Nina's room, staring straight ahead. She caught Danny and Jim in her peripheral vision, but she wasn't sure what they were doing or exactly where they were standing. She realized she was holding her breath as she walked. This had now become her standard way to gear up for action. It made her feel powerful. She shut the door as soon as she got into Nina's bedroom.

Lise borrowed another pair of Nina's jeans, also taking a pair of underwear. She put on her own bra and Danny's cowboy shirt, feeling close to him. She stared at her damp sneakers and wondered what she could wear. Nina had enormous feet. Jen the landlady was right. It was good to have shoes on in case you had to go somewhere fast.

In the living room she saw Danny was standing, leaning against the wall where the TV was supposed to hang. Jim sat in a hard chair that was pulled up to a table, looking through sketches on scraps of paper. Lise felt ready.

"Did Nina draw these?" Jim asked.

"They're tattoo designs." She was keenly aware of Danny watching, trying to figure out what was going on.

"Nina had tattoos?" Jim addressed the pages in front of him.

"She had some small ones, the usual girl stuff. A four-leaf clover, a rose, her name." She was lying again.

"The usual?" Jim didn't seem to understand the range of options.

Lise moved into the room and sat on the couch, completing an ill-defined geometry with the two men. "She was thinking about a big one. Something on her arm and back maybe. She didn't tell me what. Maybe guys in her unit, important dates, places." More lies, she didn't know why.

"Do you have tattoos?" Jim looked at Lise now. Danny straightened up, pulling himself away from the wall.

"No," she said. She had scars. Danny leaned back against the wall in a kind of relief as she finished the thought.

"What's S-Y-O-T-O-S?" asked Jim. "Why would she want that on her body? Is it someone's name?"

She felt heavy in the cushions and lifted herself out of the couch and into the large chair. It felt good to sit in it, to draw her legs under her body, to hold onto the arm rests and feel something was holding her.

She had told Danny about this, but didn't want to tell Jim what the letters meant.

Danny spoke. "It's probably for the boyfriend. He's that kind of guy, right, Lise? Not Nina, she's more about the here and now, right?"

Lise felt Danny's gift and she was amazed. She stared at him, wanting to look into his eyes for once, but he looked away. Then she remembered he was just quoting her.

Jim didn't say anything and then folded the drawings in half, the clean sides of the paper on the outside. He searched and found a pen in his jacket pocket.

"She's run away. Now we look for her."

Lise was relieved. He was going to move forward. He believed. They would find her.

"We'll do it just like on TV. What did Nina do, where did she work? Who are her friends? Who saw her last?"

Jim held his pen over the folded tattoo drawings and looked from Lise to Danny, waiting for answers.

Lise told him about the acting class Nina took, about the waitress job she had for a few lunchtime shifts, about the story meetings at Danny's producer's office in Culver City, about the sessions at Nik's, about the landlady's daughter and how Nina had babysat for her a few times, about the nights drinking at the Buccaneer and getting high in the parking lot. Lise told him about Nina's guy, but didn't mention he was a sniper. It still seemed like scary information.

"You do this movie storytelling too?" Jim asked after Lise's longish, mostly true story. "That how you know this guy?" He jerked his head to Danny.

Lise answered quickly. "Danny's working on a screenplay. I'm giving him details, technical advisor stuff."

"It's how it's done. With certain subject matter," Danny added.

Lise realized she was being forced to choose sides.

Danny explained research and writing to Jim. Lise wanted to find a place to hide until Jim's impatient slightly-homicidal look dissolved or Danny stopped talking—whichever happened first. When Danny got to the part about how Lise told her Green Zone stories to him, all she heard was cash-and-carry not blood-and-guts. Jim seemed insulted as well and looked at the wood planks of the floor, gently shaking his head at the short-comings Danny related.

"How do you know if you're getting it right?" Jim asked Danny. "You being a civilian."

Lise and Jim waited for the answer.

"I'll go over and see if Jen has a pair of flip-flops that might fit you," Danny said. And then Lise and Jim were alone, waiting for the screen door to slam back into place.

"Did Nina say why she joined the army?"

"We don't talk about it that way."

"Did she join because of her father, because he died in nine-eleven?"

"It's more about what she got out of it."

"Is it the same for you? Was it the same for you?"

"I wanted something—rules, something to keep me in line."

"It's not always inside us, I guess."

"I think Nina wanted to be harder."

"Harder? Like tough, in shape?"

"Nik talks about it better."

"I think I need to meet this Nik."

"Nina's backpack is at his place. We could go get it, look in it. Maybe there's something."

"Great. We can go then."

"Talking with him is interesting."

"When he's not being a dick?"

"It always feels like a good conversation."

"What does he say about being harder?"

"Civilians are soft."

"Do you buy that?"

"Not sure I understand it totally. Not sure how I can apply it."

"Why do you screw up words?"

"Got hit in the head in Iraq. Lots of alphabet soup for what I have. Sometimes I'm slow or mixed up. It's hard to notice."

"Thanks for sharing."

"You in AA?"

"A couple of years. Obvious, huh?"

"Sorry about the bar before."

"You do what you need to, don't worry about me."

"What was Nina's dad like?"

"Ryan? He was—what do they say—good people? Nice, smart, but not a show-off."

"Like you?"

"I was always trying to prove something. I didn't listen. Ryan listened. He didn't make as much money."

"You made a lot of money."

"Maybe."

They hadn't been looking at each other as they spoke. Lise wondered if maybe she was just talking to herself.

"Nina went AWOL for a couple of days about three weeks ago. Turned out it was a road trip with someone in the producer's office. They went up the coast, did the drive on Route 1."

"What's AWOL mean if it's just a weekend getaway?"

"People need to stay in touch."

"Why?"

"Because of how we are."

"So maybe she's not missing just because people are freaking out wondering where she is."

"It's been three days."

"So it's not just you and people like you freaking out?"

Lise didn't know how to answer this. "Do you still make money back in the real world?"

"I'm not sure. There was something on the news this morning and then I heard a report on a radio at some point today—something's happening. Like I said, I really do need to watch some TV news for a while, catch up and see what's happening in civilization."

"This is civilization."

"This is the second longest day of my life. Can we go to Nik's and look through Nina's backpack?"

"She'll need it when we find her."

"This day is getting longer."

"I don't really sleep."

## ELEVEN

Jen and Danny were sunk deep in the couch, numbed by numbers, abbreviations and hysterical talking heads thundering at them from CNN. Jen had the feeling she was watching the fourth quarter of a lengthy, dull Super Bowl after eight hours of pre-game programming. She felt dried out and migraine-y. Everyone was shouting, saying how important this was, how terrible, how amazing. *Unprecedented, literally without precedent.* She knew all the reporters wanted to scream "what the fuck", throw down their microphones and cover their ears so they wouldn't have to hear someone explain for the ten thousandth time what was happening with this thing you couldn't even see. It was more dominoes falling.

Marco came in and stood by the edge of the couch, not talking, just absorbing the lights and sounds of the television.

"We're fucked, you know that?" Marco looked from Jen to Danny. "Hey, Dan, how's it going?"

Danny grunted back at him.

"We'll never unload that condo now. Not to mention the total financial shit hole we're in."

"Maybe Danny doesn't need to hear about our finances," Jen said, starting to feel something pointed under her anxiety. *Heard the one about the woman with two husbands?*

"Everybody's in the same boat now," Marco said and left the

room.

"How fucked is fucked, do you think?" Jen asked Danny. Her New York tone came back whenever she saw him. They had this in common. She doubted she or Danny talked this way to anyone else they knew in California.

"Depends. Maybe he's right."

"I thought you were my friend."

"I'm sure it's all good."

"We're out of beer. Is there any next door?"

"Not sure. It's a house full of crazy over there."

She liked that Danny kept up with the thoughts caroming in her brain, "Lise and Nina's uncle? His name's Jim, right?" Jen wasn't sure if she wanted to see him, to see if she remembered correctly, to see if he remembered at all. *Hi, nice to meet you. Have we fucked before?*

"I don't get it—people carrying their shit around in full display twenty-four-seven. This isn't that hard."

"What, life? Yeah, it is, Danny Boy. Grow the fuck up. I say this with love." More New York, like she was an old Irish guy sitting at a bar. *Another Jameson, dearie.*

"Every minute is like a page-one rewrite with this girl. It's too extreme."

"She was an army nurse who took guys' limbs off. What is she, like, thirty? I don't think she qualifies as a girl."

"You know what I mean."

"You love all her drama, gives you street cred." Jen decided to take her own advice. "Let's go over there and face the music." Thinking Danny offered protection was a mistake, but maybe it was enough.

Jen knew this was a bad idea. As they walked the fifteen feet to the rental house, she thought of turning back at least four times. Even as they were crossing the doorway, entering the living room, she was thinking, *this is a bad—really bad—idea.*

Jim looked up at her as she entered the room and his look told her everything. He remembered her, knew exactly who she was. *Maybe.*

She watched him start to replay their time together, just for an instant, and then she saw him shove it down and away far from the space they occupied now. But she wasn't completely sure what she saw. Jen knew it made her feel rejected, slapped down, even as her bad-girl-on-a-bender desire blossomed. So this is what a money guy looks like with a few more years on him—unrested and enraged.

Lise looked to Danny, who made introductions.

"Jim, Jen Broder. Jen, Jim Wicklow. Jen's the landlady. Jim's the uncle." Danny sounded like he was reading out roles in a screenplay.

"It's nice to meet you. Shitty circumstances." Jen felt herself smile and move toward him. She watched him fumble himself up out of the chair.

They hesitantly extended hands to each other and made rushed eye contact. Their hands dropped almost immediately after they shook and Jen felt an intense desire to scratch her palm, but thought it wouldn't seem cool.

"You're Diana's friend?" Jen wasn't sure who Jim meant to say this to. He wouldn't look into her face.

"I'm her second cousin's cousin twice-removed or some nonsense."

Jen watched him try to connect the dots, but fail utterly.

"It's not a big deal," Jen said. "I'm not really family. I'm just who Diana called when Nina needed a place to stay that wasn't in New York." She immediately tired of his bobbing and weaving. "I'm sorry, but you look familiar. Did we know each other in New York? Did Diana ever introduce us or something else?" Doubt gripped her suddenly and she added, "Maybe?"

Comprehension lit up a part of Danny's brain and Jen saw the beginning of that weird Danny-smile out of the corner of her eye. She knew he was sifting through a likely backstory for the Uncle and the Friend.

"You know, maybe." Jim said, putting on a gentleman's affect, although Jen wasn't buying.

"I mean, all New Yorkers look familiar."

Jim lowered his voice, trying to talk just to Jen. "I wasn't in great shape for a while there so the memories are a little blurry, if you know what I mean."

She wasn't sure if this was an admission or not. He was talking about time. He was talking about himself.

"Hey, we're all adults. It's only rock and roll, right?" Jen forced a cool cheerfulness. She felt high-school stupid and worried that she had said this all at top volume.

Jim and Jen both smiled with relief that they had survived this encounter. Jen was sure Danny was exhilarated by all this intrigue. She looked past Jim to Lise, who sat in a chair, staring at her bare feet, disconnected.

"Mia says hi, Captain Lise."

Lise looked up and smiled a stranger-smile at her.

"Shoes?" Lise asked, her face flashing as she remembered Jen.

"Oh shit," this was Danny, forgetting the one thing again. "Lise, Jen—shit." His owly head swiveled from one woman to the other. "Lise needs shoes. That's why I came over."

Everything slowed as they all waited for an answer to Lise's poorly asked question. Jen didn't want to be standing where she was and she didn't want to go back to her own house. She wanted to ask if there was beer in Nina's fridge. She wanted to have a private moment of lust or anger with Jim, but he wasn't letting her in and her husband was storming next door, hopefully keeping guard over her child, but also lying in wait for his wife. The thoughts formed with clarity, the words came together and she dropped her shoulders away from her ears and down her back.

"Sure, not a problem. I'm sure they'll fit. I'll go grab a pair."

The sounds of the world started up again around her as she made her way back to her home. It was as if the volume had been turned down and now someone was turning it up.

Her house was still and seemed unoccupied, but somehow was screaming at her. She found Marco at the kitchen table, reading a magazine she didn't recognize. He was barely breathing. He didn't look up as she walked by. She checked on Mia, peering into the fishbowl glow of her daughter's room. The little girl had wrapped her bed covers in a swirly twist around her legs and was on her side, arms flung out, mouth slack, sleeping the sleep of seven-year-olds.

Jen pawed through the bottom of her closet and found an old pair of Nikes she didn't wear anymore. She had no idea what size Lise wore, but for some reason it had been decided that Jen's shoes would fit.

She sat on the edge of the bed and scratched at non-existent itches on her head. She felt as if she was failing in an extremely alliterative manner—money, Marco and Mia. She didn't have the expertise to solve these things. Her New York survival skills, her young urban professional experience, her inner resources, which she was fairly sure now had never developed—all of these seemed to exist at such a great distance, no longer at her disposal. She could barely do the math.

Who the hell was on her side? Marco? Hardly. Mia? Not if she was smart. Danny? What use was that? She should have been the one to run away. Is that even what Nina had done—run away or gone away?

The house noise came on louder now. She could hear Mia breathing in bed, straining against the tortured twist of her sheets. She could hear Marco turn a glossy page, fold it over and reach for a sip of whatever he was drinking. Had he turned on the radio or was the music she heard coming from the rental house? What made a good soundtrack for what was happening? *We're taking requests.* They had plenty of music in various forms in the house and she couldn't think of any song titles or band names.

"You okay?" Marco stood in the doorway, holding his rolled up magazine in one fist.

"Do you hear that? There's music."

"It's probably from up the street. The blue house is always playing something bad too loudly."

"I thought it sounded nice. Do you know what it is?"

"I can't hear it."

"I don't want to fight."

"Talking isn't always fighting."

"The way you do it is."

"We have to sit down and count our pennies and make a plan."

"I can't deal with this right now."

"She's barely a relative, she's barely a tenant. I'm sympathetic, but we have our own shit to deal with."

"I feel responsible."

"Feel responsible about your own shit."

"This means something to me. Something is happening."

"Not everything's an emergency."

"This is happening."

Marco's presence felt threatening as he came closer, moving three strides across the room to her. He sat beside her on the bed. He dropped the magazine and pulled her awkwardly to his chest. She neither resisted nor complied.

"I need you to be in this with me," he mouthed into her hair. "We need to sit down and look at the statements and add shit up and make decisions and maybe get different jobs and sell shit and maybe move and really fix this not just for now but for a long time."

Jen's mind blanked out.

Marco kissed her firmly where he could find skin. He pressed her down on the bed and put his hands on her and tried to find her mouth with his. She lay heavy under him, shifting her body in direct opposition to his. Their clothes rubbed and rolled until she found the experience unbearable and asked him to stop.

"It hurts, this hurts. I don't want you on me. This hurts."

He shoved himself up and away from her.

In his patient explaining tone, he said, "It's love, Jen."

Outside in the nighttime streets of Sierra Madre, Jen could smell the wild fire in the hills above her. Tiny bits of ash landed on her arms, smudging in the moisture of her skin. She peered through the windows of the rental house. She saw three characters in a play, talking past each other, grateful for the in-between silences. She wasn't going back in there. She knocked on the door jamb, dropped the Nikes to the welcome mat and fled.

The sidewalk jammed up through each thigh as she stomped

down the hill toward town. Jen heard her own breathing amid the noise of passing cars and the muttering of TVs inside the houses on Baldwin. Her feet shifted on the rubber of her flip-flops, the smack of the shoe hitting her heels was slightly out of sync with her breathing. The Starbucks was closed, but she could sense things were hopping behind the closed door of the Buccaneer. She realized she had no money or cards on her. The night made her feel that no one could see her despite the fact she was in full view of pedestrians and drivers.

Suddenly the Valero station across the street offered promise. The light turned green and she crossed. She walked toward the gas pumps feeling like she was breaking a rule by not having a tank that needed filling. She looked at the holstered nozzles, wondering what it would feel like to hold one and just stand there with no car to put it in. As Jen entered the store part of the station, the young clerk looked up and gave Jen a lifted chin of recognition and greeting and went back to reading her textbook. How many times had Jen been in here? She registered the security mirror up in the corner of the store and remembered she had been an expert shoplifter in grade school, just slightly older than Mia was now—the beginning of her fun years. *The Mod Squad* trading cards, Wacky Packages and Milky Way bars. She couldn't imagine her daughter wanting to be a criminal mastermind.

Jen wandered the short aisles of the store wondering what to take. She usually bought gum or milk or beer here, but only if she was also getting gas. There were too many choices so she just grabbed a Drake's Cherry Fruit Pie and shoved it in the waist of her jeans and pulled her shirt layers over it. She dropped her arm over the bulge and looked to the clerk. She was still reading. Jen strolled quickly to the cold cases. She pulled open a door, grabbed a beer bottle from a six-pack carton and shoved it into the back pocket of her jeans. It was incredibly cold and she swallowed a yelp. She strode up to the clerk's counter—her breath slightly out of reach, her heart blipping erratically—and asked for a pack of Marlboros.

"Reds?" The clerk asked, without taking her eyes off the diagram on page 84.

"Lights, please. 100s," Jen said, surprised to hear her voice steady and slow.

The clerk re-focused, grabbed the right pack and slid it over to Jen.

"Oh, shit," Jen said, just as she'd practiced in her head. "I left my cash in the car. Be right back."

Jen walked out of the store convinced the studious clerk would notice the beer in her pocket, but something in her sensed that the clerk had simply dropped her eyes back to the page of her book. Jen heard the glass door close behind her and she kept walking across the weirdly lit station lot, past the pumps and the signs. She crossed the intersection at a diagonal as the pedestrian light flashed with caution, and then started back up the hill.

She wanted to eat the pie and drink the beer right away, but she denied herself until she reached her street. She stood opposite the property watching for movement in the two houses, slowing her breathing. She didn't see Marco or Mia in the dark of her own house, but through the trees she could see shadows crossing the lit windows of the rental house. She wondered if Lise had gotten the sneakers.

She sat on the curb between two parked cars and ate the pie. It was disgusting, papery and processed. She finished it all, sucking on her fingers to get the stickiness off them. The burnt air swirled around her and her skin felt coated with microscopic debris from the canyon fires. She had set the beer on the asphalt while she ate the pie and before she reached for it she worried that it wouldn't be a twist-off, but it was. Thank you, Mr. Bud Light. It was thin gruel as beers go, but it washed her mouth of the manufactured sweet and made her feel like a cool villain getting ready to pull another heist. The problem was—if the screaming televisions were to be believed—there were no more banks to rob.

## TWELVE

Jim zipped up his fly and turned to the sink to wash his hands. His dripping wet fingers reached for a towel that wasn't there. He stood frozen, arms suspended in the air. His body was so tired, his mind so filled with roaring chaos, that he simply paused in space in Nina's bathroom until the hot, sooty air dried his hands.

It was the middle of the night when he started this journey and now it was again the middle of the night. Was it twenty-four hours or forty-eight since this all had started, since the bleating cell in the night, since the extended emergency began? He'd made mistakes, but he had made decisions too, focused on a task. He was rising to the occasion. He felt cowed by his stupid pass at the strange girl, but also found confidence in helping her get cleaned up. He had a glimpse of her small thin breasts as she slipped under the bubbles and he was both relieved and worried that it hadn't turned him on. Go to this Nik's house, look through the backpack, find Nina.

Jim, Lise and Danny closed up the house, shutting the windows against the heated air. Jim was quietly pleased he wouldn't have to see Jen again when he saw the sneakers she had left for Lise. He watched Lise shove her feet into them and then they walked toward the street and into the night.

"My car?" Danny asked. "I'm parked up the street."

"The way to Nik's is tricky," Lise told him.

Jim wondered about curving climbing roads in the deepening dark.

"Can't believe I get to meet the famous Nik." Danny was excited and turned his face to Jim to show it.

Jim simply nodded as if someone had instructed him to not speak.

"Let's take my Jetta. His stuff is in my trunk."

Jim was glad Lise was thinking about his belongings. He had completely forgotten them.

The three of them set off for Lise's car. Jim trailed behind, following, watching their backs as Danny muttered to Lise. He probably didn't want Jim there. Jim noticed a notepad sticking out of Danny's back pocket. Was the screenwriter going to take notes?

As soon as Jim slid into the Jetta's backseat he lost what little nerve he had gained. Night permeated everything and there didn't seem to be enough streetlights for them to see the way. The car's headlights revealed—and only at the last minute—whatever was ahead of them, and Jim felt threatened by the darkness to the side and behind him. He wanted three-sixty illumination and it was not in the offing.

Jim looked at the back of Lise's head as she drove them up into the canyon. His sense of purpose and direction seeped from him. He felt powerless and overwhelmed again and gave himself over to whoever Lise was and wherever she was taking him. This Nik person and his home now loomed dangerously in Jim's mind. This wasn't going to be good. He deeply felt he was at risk. He should probably find an AA meeting instead of retrieving Nina's lost backpack at some war freak's house in the middle of the night. He should probably find a TV and find out what had been happening in the world. He should probably call Sarah.

Cars streamed toward them, bright headlights lighting up the inside of the Jetta each time they passed. He was supposed to be searching for Nina, the errand to retrieve her backpack at Nik's was supposed to serve that mission. But Jim felt he was traveling in the wrong direction now, not toward a solution to his niece's disappearance but straight into the fire. He had run away before, while men in uniforms went past him the opposite way—away from safety.

"What's with all the traffic?" Jim half-shouted from the back seat.

Lise said something he didn't quite catch about mountain people and fire. He wondered why no one in the car was concerned about the direction they were traveling. He also wondered why he wasn't thinking about the fact the driver of this car had been drinking. He pushed a button on the armrest and his window slid down a few inches. He smelled smoke. The window slid back up, controlled by someone in the front seat.

The conversations at the VA came back to him. Soldiers had gotten lost at home and the military and local police were looking for them. This comforted Jim: Nina wasn't alone. But what if she wasn't with the others? Was this half-assed search party in the Jetta the only people looking for Nina? He couldn't shake this needling concern that war was everywhere, didn't end or begin, even when you came home. This idea increased his loss of direction.

Nina must have killed people, seen dead bodies certainly, lost people to death—watched as they slipped from living to the other thing. Anxiety seized him from inside and he worried about his own death, about Sarah's, about his children's. The fear left him as quickly as it had come. He had never seen a dead body. He hadn't seen his father's or mother's (was it on purpose, he wondered now) and Ryan's body had never been found. He saw no other bodies on that day, although he must have passed them in the street or felt them land as they jumped-fell from above him. That day felt so informed by death, but not by dead bodies. Had he refused to look or had he seen them and let them go?

Jim adjusted his sights to stare at the back of Danny's head. This skinny Hollywood fucker—probably by way of suburban New Jersey—was a familiar type to Jim. He had not appreciated the dressing down he had received from this screenwriter, getting all mouthy with him, standing in a semi-threatening way as if he might know some kind of martial art. Danny hadn't said the specific words standing in that living room, but Jim had heard him loud and clear. Back off Lise. In the end, Danny's threats didn't matter. Jim had lost that kind of desire somewhere during the course of this day—even the pass had simply been an attempt to locate lust—and he was now unable to take any steps of his own. He was being carried along, propelled upward, deeper into the darkness, dreading every turn they made.

They had been driving in heavy silence for some time when Jim remembered events had been leaking toward him all day in snatches of nervous announcements and news. Something was happening in the money system and he hoped learning details would anchor him.

"Do you think we could turn on the radio? I'd like to hear the news."

Danny whirled around in his seat, constrained by the shoulder harness of the seat belt. "What was that?"

Jim repeated himself, unsure what rule he was breaking.

Lise switched on the radio and twirled the station knob searching for something clear within the static of the mountains. Jim heard snatches of music, religion and announcers. Something about Lehman Brothers that he couldn't quite hear was delivered with the hysterical tones usually reserved for recapping the apocalypse. He heard the words "down" and "worst." Had the cracks split wide open? Could they even do that? Is this what he had heard snatches of all day, in the airport, in that bar? Lise shut off the radio when she couldn't find a clear signal. Jim looked through the window glass and saw himself reflected back.

And the woman from New York. Just thinking about her made him feel as if he was cheating on Sarah, although they hadn't even met yet during his days of dark nights. This woman—Jen, he had been told—either way, he wasn't exactly sure who she was. Though he knew what she might have been.

After his shock had thawed somewhat at the end of 2001, he went to work trying to destroy himself. It was how friends of his had gotten through college—four years of ruination leading to a bright future. He had also tried to prove to himself that he wasn't dead by relentlessly having sex with as many willing women he could find in bars, restaurants, private parties and, twice, toward the end of his downhill run, with a high-end Natasha in a room at the Soho Grand. And once with his ex-wife in the backseat of her Lexus in the driveway of the Westchester house she had gotten in the divorce. She hadn't wanted J.J. and Emily to know he was there.

Jen might've been early on in all of this—if she'd been at all—after the drunken yelling matches with New York's educated women who pleaded with him not to blame Islam just these guys. Jim remembered screaming, while ordering another round, that he wasn't blaming anyone, why weren't they listening to him, and did they want to go somewhere else for just one more. This communal scream-drinking lasted months, maybe years.

He never saved phone numbers, never remembered addresses, and banished names from his mind. He called women "baby" and "girl" and channeled early Springsteen lyrics in each gesture of intimacy. Every encounter was intense and serious and hinted at epic meaning. He wasn't faking it. Sex then felt very much like his life depended on it.

Jen might've been one of those girl-women. The way she had coolly looked at him in Nina's rented house, how he had found himself physically familiar with her in just that brief handshake. He had vague memories of someone who looked like her babbling, filled with other people's words even as he held her, kissed her, turned her toward him. She seemed to be an oracle, spouting nonsense and news. In the shreds of his nighttime memory he had found ballast and connection in her noise. Or someone who looked like her.

Lise brought the car to a stop and pulled the handbrake.

"We're here," she said.

Jim would make progress now. And although the hovering, looming mystery of Nik made Jim unsure of himself, he knew this was a place with a connection to the wider world. Nik would have a television.

The heated scent of fire hit Jim as soon as he opened the car door. He followed Lise and Danny on foot up the drive to the front door of a low-slung house. Danny bounced on the balls of his feet.

The heavy wood door opened and Nik stood backlit in the doorway. He looked just as Jim had imagined he would. As Lise explained who everyone was and why they were there, Nik nodded his head and looked severe. A thin halo of light formed around Nik's Jagger-like hair as he vibrated before them.

"Welcome welcome, writer boy and Specialist Wicklow's Uncle Jim. Come on in. Captain Sheridan, show them the way."

Jim followed the others across the threshold, wondering if he were to take any of the drugs that Nik was obviously on—or what he had pilfered from Nina's bathroom—if it would count and send him back to Day One at AA. He also wondered how long he could wait before asking if he could turn on a screen, any screen.

"Uncle Jim, come in." Nik slapped Jim on the shoulder as he passed. "Sorry, no American Express accepted here, man. We're all out of credit. It's end times for money, baby."

# BROKEN WORLD

## THIRTEEN

If Jim hadn't caught some of the fragments of financial news rushing toward him all day long, he would have assumed this was just another fool taking a shot at people like him, but the gleam reflecting off Nik's dilated pupils sent Jim's pulse throbbing and he couldn't find his breath.

"Is something happening?" He knew he was asking the wrong person. He also knew the answer. He'd had a feeling for months that something enormous was on its way. When it turned out to be Nina gone missing, he thought he had been waiting for the wrong thing, that the bad thing had come, and it was more personal than he expected. But ever since he had landed in this place he'd felt something else—something huge and devouring—hovering over them all.

"Oh man. You are definitely going to need some quality TV time."

Yes, Jim desperately wanted that television—something he could control, something that gave him the information he needed. He thought of the flat screen that lay dead on the floor of Nina's house. He thought of his own dead screens at home on the Cape. If he had only consulted them more often—then what?

But Maxwell and Acevedo would not give up the television. They were in the middle of a heated duel in *Call of Duty IV* and were not to be disturbed by some guy they didn't know who wanted to watch CNBC.

"War heroes, Uncle Jim," Nik said. "Veterans of the armed forces get priority around here. Uncle Sam before Uncle Jim." Nik clucked his tongue to communicate who was the victor. He seemed to have been saving up material for this night's performance. Lise and Danny faded into the background and Jim felt alone with a lunatic.

"Where's my niece's backpack?" Maybe he could call a cab and get out of there on his own. He could grab Nina's stuff and get to a hotel and a TV. He was starting to think, his survival instincts kicking in, but there was something about Nik that shut him down, made him forget as soon as he remembered. Ryan would've known how to handle this guy, put a hand on his shoulder, persuade him.

"Yes, let's get the backpack and have a talk while the boys finish their game."

Jim followed Nik and Lise and Danny into the kitchen all the while trying to pin down what was really bothering him about the kids slamming away on the videogame controls. Jesus, it hit him: they had only three arms between them.

The four of them stood in the kitchen. Jim managed to decline the offer of a beer, but Nik placed a sweaty open bottle in front of him anyway. Jim watched the others wet their dry mouths with the sweet liquid. The patio door was open and the scent of fire was very strong.

"We have an evacuation order for midnight, but I don't usually leave. Fire came pretty close three years ago. Some guys and I stayed, fought the fucker. County boys tried to order us out, but there's a lot of stuff here that's not exactly portable under the watchful eye of the G. Know what I mean?"

Jim did not know what Nik meant, but he was transfixed listening to his language. Jim saw Danny reach for something in his back pocket, but Lise held his arm in place and wouldn't let him move. Jim worried he was standing at the epicenter of a criminal enterprise. There were probably weapons and drugs stashed in the house.

"Specialist Nina Wicklow is good people, Uncle Jim," Nik said this staring into Jim's eyes as if he was placing ideas in his head. "War is not healthy for children and other living things, isn't that right?"

"Yes," Jim said. "Listen, uh, Nik—"

"—Yes, Uncle Jim?" Nik cut him off as if he was trying to redirect him to some other path.

"Can I get Nina's backpack?"

Lise held up the pack so Jim could see it. It seemed unremarkable for something that he suddenly felt he was risking his life for. Jim took the backpack and slung it over one shoulder. He could feel there was almost nothing in it. He thought about finding some place quiet very soon, sitting down and sifting gently through its contents.

There was shouting from the living room and then Maxwell came in and grabbed the open beer from in front of Jim. "Game over sir. You can watch your program now."

They found places around the TV. Nik held the remote and switched the input and channel, moving the game equipment out of the way. They all watched Jim watch CNN.

It was well after midnight in the East and Jim could tell that the anchorman was having a very long day. There was a lot of information and Jim had trouble following at first, feeling as if he had been dropped into the middle. Data crawled along the bottom and headlines and sub-headlines were supered above that. There was a special side graphic that showed the market's alarming descent of five hundred four points. The anchorman recapped and then interviewed a series of experts before recapping again. Jim watched, expressionless, feeling little except the sensation that he was suspended in mid-air, unable to fly and unwilling to fall.

Bank of America had bought Merrill Lynch, saved it, what was left of it. He'd been out of the loop for so long that this kind of transaction seemed impossible. But then he remembered Bear Stearns had been bought in March by JP Morgan Chase. Lehman Brothers had failed, was filing for bankruptcy. This rattled Jim even more. The government hadn't saved Lehman. He felt too rusty and too fogged to sort through all these events—figure out what was good, bad, right, wrong. He wasn't even completely sure of the positions he currently held. One thing he could grasp: there might not be anyone to save them.

He could imagine bankers and traders alike flipping out. He could see the screamers screaming and the guys who put their heads in their hands, doing just that. He'd forgotten which one he had been. Bond guys were usually quiet, murmuring softly into their phones, but his instincts told him that hadn't been him.

There had been some kind of uncontrolled system-wide failure that jumped from one circuit to another. It was all so interconnected that if one failed, the rest would go too—one company, then another, one country, then another. There was no one to save you.

The world was ending. Not with the bang of a nuclear bomb, but with the whimpering bleat of an unanswered phone. Even if someone had answered the call, there would have been nothing on the other end.

Jim finally spoke: "Fuck me."

Nik laughed and then added, "That would be about right."

Danny freed his arm from Lise's grip and started demolishing a notebook page by page with frantic pen scribbles he would never be able to read. Lise retreated to join Maxwell and Acevedo in the kitchen doorway and accepted another beer to suck down.

"I need to make a call." Jim gripped his cell phone, knowing he sounded a little hysterical.

"Cell reception's better outside," Nik said helpfully.

Jim stepped out into the night and slammed into the hot air. How close was this fire that they were not running from? He opened his phone and saw the bars float alive. He pushed the single button he had programmed to connect him to home. He heard the ringing and anticipated Sarah groggily interrupting it. The ringing continued. He counted rings, turned to face the house and watched the people move around inside the lighted rooms.

Danny interviewed Nik in the kitchen. He kept moving his new Apple phone from his mouth to Nik's, recording what they said. Lise joined Maxwell and Acevedo on the couch, sitting between them as they resumed the videogame. The ground lurched up at Jim and he wondered if he was going to vomit, but he swallowed the horror back down. He yearned for what was lost—people, opportunities, money. He wanted years returned to him in the condition in which they had begun. He wondered if he had brought this on himself then flung the thought away. An invisible hand pressed down on him from within and he felt as if he was choking.

He focused on what he needed to do and managed to dial Sarah's cell phone from memory. He turned away from the lit house, faced the darkness of the woods.

"Where the fuck are you?" Jim didn't mean to sound angry. "And why are you awake?"

"Nice to hear from you too, asshole," Sarah shot right back at him without taking a breath. "I'm awake because things are happening that are keeping me from sleeping—like my husband calling in the middle of the night."

They breathed at each other for a few moments.

"Let's start over," Jim offered.

"Are you okay?"

"Where are you? I called the house."

"I'm at Bill and Mark's. After I talked to you—I was trying to tell you earlier what was happening, but you needed to focus on other things. I just felt separate from everyone. And the news finally sank in—what was going on and it all got so weird—it just felt like everything was ending. I didn't want to be alone. I took the bus here. I didn't think I could drive. And I had this crazy thought that I might get car-jacked by, you know, other people."

This seemed impossible to Jim—that his wife would take the bus along the Cape.

"Are we okay? Financially, I mean."

"We're fine." He doubted it—how could they be—if this continued. "We're diversified." The word sounded feeble to his ear.

"That's what Bill and Mark said too."

Jim felt he was being second-guessed even as he lied.

Sarah continued her quiet, urgent explanations. "It wasn't just today or yesterday. It's been happening. Did you know?" Jim won-

dered about how to answer this. He thought about the joke about
the guy, when asked how he'd gone bankrupt, answered: slowly and
then all at once.

"Babe, I'm sorry," Sarah said. "I'm having trouble with per-
spective. You're out there doing this brave thing and I'm here worrying about money, feeling like it's the end of the world when it's
probably just about other people. Are you okay?"

Jim had no idea how he was and he had forgotten the specific
reason he had given himself for calling. He wanted to tell her that
he'd been in a bar, that he'd made a pass at a woman, and that he was
in the home of a probably-armed, definitely-stoned, freak-preacher
who had survived Vietnam and the rest of the sixties and would
likely survive whatever was next.

"Who's in charge?" Jim hadn't thought to ask this. The words
emerged fully spoken and he couldn't take them back. He realized that's what he hadn't found out from CNN. That's what they
couldn't report.

Sarah said she couldn't hear him, he was breaking up. Jim
shouted her name over and over, but he was really asking the question again in his head. She shouted back and their names crossed in
the air somewhere between cell towers. The call dropped and Jim
closed his phone. His will receded, out to sea.

It was the lack of sleep, the time-zone change, the strange people home from war, the woman he had maybe fucked all those years
ago, the missing niece he barely knew and the still hemorrhaging loss
of Ryan—this litany of Shit That Is Wrong, he blamed all this for
his near-psychotic response to the financial news. He pulled the pill
bottle from Nina's out of his jacket pocket, but he couldn't read the
label. He was afraid to swallow something he couldn't name.

There was a commotion in the house. A red light swept across
everything and then vanished, only to reappear again, turning the
color of the scene on and then off. Everyone converged on the front
door. Jim moved into the house, clutching his phone, asked what
was going on. The red light didn't feel like anything when it bathed
his face. Someone banged loudly on the door.

"That's a government knock," Maxwell said.

"The G is into no-knock these days, but I believe you are correct, soldier." Nik had a line for everything, like the screenwriter was feeding him dialogue.

Nik opened the door to a sheriff's deputy with a clipboard and pen.

"Time to go, folks," the deputy announced. "We've got to get you out earlier. Fire's moving fast. Everybody in the upper canyon has got to go and got to go now."

"Think we'll stick it out, Deputy." Maxwell and Acevedo stood erect behind Nik as he said this.

"C'mon. You people resist every fire season. This house is about fifteen minutes from being barbequed. So no hassles. Grab your valuables, vital records, family photos and let's go."

There was a long moment when it seemed there was a standoff and then Nik accepted the deputy's orders. He turned to his guests and told everyone to grab their stuff, get in their cars.

"And those with nowhere to go?" Nik addressed the clipboard more than the deputy.

"Red Cross is set up at St. Rita's on Baldwin down the hill." The deputy flipped the pages on his clipboard and added, "Safe evacuation, please." And then he was gone. A few moments later the red light that had bathed them all was gone as well.

Jim piled back into the Jetta with Lise and Danny. He held Nina's backpack in his lap. He looked out the back window and watched Nik and the other two load up an old truck with duffle bags and a long metal box. He didn't want to see anymore and was glad when Lise started the car and they pulled away.

"The Red Cross'll need help. There may be sick people." There was something bright in Lise's voice. There was something more whole about her.

"I'm good. We can go home later." Danny tried to sound neutral, but he seemed filled with newness as well.

The Jetta fell in with the stream of other cars moving down the winding hill in a slow procession. Jim was going in the right direction now and at the end of the journey there would be a place to lay his head and rest. He remembered now he had been a screamer. That was why he had needed Ryan, the guy who picked up the pieces after the screamers screamed.

## FOURTEEN

Lise recited her credentials to a Red Cross administrator who put her to work. Through the night she accumulated tools: stethoscope, gloves, robotic reassurance. She touched every person she was presented with, feeling all their limbs to make sure they were still there and would remain. It became compulsive, an obsessive tic she couldn't control, but it made her look like she was providing care.

There were old men and old women—more than she expected. The women reminded her of the ones in Denver. It was always these tough old broads who came into the St. Anthony ER, these Western women who didn't like being sick or hurt or requiring assistance. In St. Rita's she touched and helped everyone, old and young, men and women, husbands and wives with children they were no longer interested in, from whom they wanted a respite. Lise gave them relief, giving them bottled water, telling them they were tired and should try to sleep. The kids were fine, wherever they were.

People talked to her while she examined them, which she wasn't used to. They chatted nervously, thanked her, asked who they should speak to about the fire and their homes. Did she know how long they would be evacuated? Lise nodded, grunted, told them to shush while she took their pulse, listened to their hearts, watched them breathe. Then she would push them gently down to prone positions, pressing them to sleep. These were not the arrangements of the Cash. These people were not silenced by shock, these bodies were whole.

Lise walked through the rooms. There were a few empty cots and on each was a water bottle, a sandwich wrapped in plastic and a travel-size toothpaste and a toothbrush waiting to be claimed. Television screens silently pushed colored lights into the air from the high corners of the larger rooms. Lise moved along the rows of the not-sleeping refugees, making her count, filling out the Red Cross records in the half-light as she walked, stopped to write, walked on. When she was done she handed the paperwork to an administrator, kept the pen—a new tool of her trade—and went to find a small dark place where she could sit alone and breathe herself out of crying.

Lise could feel her inside self slipping back, relieving itself of the present, of the new anchors she had tried to put in place. All the patients—who weren't even really patients—were in bed, checked and catalogued. They didn't need Lise in emergency mode. Her efficiency and competency were of no use, to them or to her. It would have been unseemly to drink anything but coffee in St. Rita's and caffeine was not nearly enough stimulant for her out-of-reach purposes. Neither Danny nor her new comrade Jim would help here either. She needed wounds and breakage. She needed action.

Chilling, accelerating memories intruded. She found a small office and sat under the desk in the dark and broke herself into pieces. Anxiety froze her, kept her from moving except for her heaving chest. She was able to take in air and there was a deep pressuring pain that she told herself was just panic and not imminent death. She made fists and released them, repeatedly, in a bad rhythm. Her skin went warm with sweat, then cold as it dried. Her arms and legs tingled. Her brain told her body that she was fine, but her body wouldn't listen and kept up its attack on her brain.

She had been like this before and she had healed herself. Maybe not healing, but an easing. But the thoughts splashed their colors in her face and she couldn't shut herself off. The feel of that rubber knee came to her again, as if she had waited for it, readied herself for it. An unstable knee fracture—what they called a rubber knee. Telling Major Beck to feel it. Her hands still cradled the gone joint as Beck slipped his hands under hers and the soldier's leg. They held the dead limb in their live hands. Beck pulled his hands away and moved off. She heard him ask for an amputation set. She couldn't move her hands from the shattered piece of human and she couldn't look at the soldier it was attached to. She turned her head as the blue cloth-wrapped surgical set was presented to Major Beck like a gift. Lise and Beck were the last link in the chain trying to keep the soldier alive. They would save him by taking away a part of him. Life over limb.

Lise could still feel the pebbled, purpled skin of that rubbery knee in her hands. She clenched her fists, then released her hands, palms up, fingers spreading. She made fists again, felt the soldier, his skin against hers. She opened her hands, handing instruments to Major Beck, moved her hands to his surgical rhythm, followed his movements, sopped up blood after he cut, undoing and then doing, lifting away what was left of the limb, laying it down. She wrapped the limb in surgical cloth, like a gift no one would want, except the soldier she had taken it from.

Lise breathed deeply in and out, letting her breath run ahead until it slowed itself and hung back with the new cadence she forced on it. Slow. Slow and in. Slow and out. Long breaths, long inhales and long exhales. In through the nose and out through the mouth. Pulling the breath down deep into her stomach, willing the bottom of her lungs to the ground, pushing the breath back up high into her head, willing it to make her tall and light. Grounded and then into flight, repeat.

She put her mouth to her palms and tried to whisper-wish it all away. It felt like she was kissing salty, dying flesh.


Later she found a teenager in a small dark office watching a violent spy movie on a portable DVD player. Lise watched along with him, sitting in the dark with their faces lit by the screen, sharing the old-school cushiony headphones, and turning up the volume until the sounds flooded through her entire body like blood in her arteries. The pace and pulse of the movie mirrored Lise's altered state and kept her from fragmenting into freak-out and collapse—it kept her shit together. Her right foot twitched under her crossed shins, her fists were clenched. They watched the movie twice, the kid dozing beside Lise while she bent over the screen, the connector band of the headphones hanging forward over her brow.

A chopper medic woke Lise in the almost-morning. She walked most of the hallway with him before she realized she was stateside at St. Rita's and not in the Cash, taking a wounded soldier from him. She rubbed her biceps to reassure herself. Both her arms were still there.

"No one gets left Sheridan no one," Nik whisper-shouted at Lise while the men nodded around her. "What are you doing about finding Specialist Wicklow?" It felt more like an intervention—except for the bottle they were passing and not sharing with her—than a support group. Did she mean intervention or interrogation? Was her language still crumbling?

They had to leave Nik's house, but that didn't hold Nik back from having a group session. Wherever he was, they were.

She found her voice, flattened. "Slight detour I'm on it we're all on it the uncle is here." She felt she was talking in the code of weighty matters, like in the spy movie. She shifted gears. "She's my friend I would like to find her I will find her." I will find Nina, all her fingers and toes.

The others talked, jagged tales jarred loose by the evacuation and fire crisis around them. Man-boys under threat, even Nik, using talk therapy as a weapon against the gripping dark. She'd heard it all before, repetitively, and was reminded that every Nik session seemed to be held in strange light, dawn or dusk, lit by televisions and open refrigerators, low-wattage bulbs. Here, the doorsill brightened with a scoop of light thrown weakly from the hall. The rest of the room was murky and dense with shadow.

The chopper medic murmured partial words and portions of the alphabet. Nik demanded full sentences. Maxwell turned on Nik. The chain of care was breaking down. Lise stood to silence them, telling them she had work to do. She didn't feel capable, but she knew the cots of hurt people were pulling at her and away from Nik and the others.

Danny was in the hall maybe waiting for her. He went right up to her and came as close to her as he could without touching her. He breathed in her face and looked her up and down, checking some mental punch list. Lise registered that he had two arms.

"I'm crashing," Danny said. "Fried. Too old for all-nighters. You still standing?"

She was obviously still on her feet, she thought, taking extra seconds to translate Danny's words into something her brain could hold. Then she had the incredible thought that he could really help her—help them—find Nina.

"How will we find her?" she asked him.

"How the fuck do I know?" he snapped. His mouth shut and his eyes went wide in immediate and enormous regret.

Lise's brain turned professional all at once. How *would* he know, this guy, this civilian. She turned, her sneakers squeaking, walking briskly away from him, his presence receding from her. Danny melted away before she turned the corner.

The room with the cots roared at her with danger. She reversed course, spinning, and then walking up stairs and out into the almost-morning of Sierra Madre. Nik was on the sidewalk—everyone she knew seemed to be waiting for her wherever she went.

"Oh fuck the backpack." Seeing Nik reminded her that they hadn't looked inside. Or maybe Jim had and he hadn't told her. Lise had to find him, find Nina. She stopped moving.

"Sheridan." Nik looked exposed and fragile in the dawn air. She needed him mysterious and strong, something to hold onto and then let go of. "There's nothing in that backpack."

"Is that like a riddle you fucking mystic?"

"You're in no shape to care for the wounded."

"There are no wounded here."

"That's all we've got."

"Why do you always start with this shit, this shit you start?" Her language was going and her limbs were tingling with icy needles. Her breath left her in great pushing rushes, the sidewalk was all she could see. Major Beck was speaking calmly, so close into one of her ears. *Slow down*. Nik and the Major, one in each ear, one on each side of her, like an angel and a devil.

She felt people—strong, lean men—carry her, take her down stairs, whoosh her though doorways and release her with as little force as they could manage onto the taut surface of an empty cot. She smelled the dank canvas and the chrome frame.

# FIFTEEN

Jim slept lightly for most of the night. Skimming along the surface of unconsciousness, he never really submerged into complete rest. At first he had just sat on the cot and fixed his eyes on the screen above. It was all local news about the fire and evacuation, but on another screen high in another corner there was CNN detailing the financial collapse. He could see that screen better if he lay down so he stretched out awkwardly. He was awash in information as he shut himself down for the night into almost-sleep.

Buildings fell in his waking dreams and he came to after a few hours, panting, wondering where he was. Some of the cots had filled up around him. The basement was partially above ground and the small high windows let in some early light. The TV screens kept those who weren't sleeping up-to-date. Jim reached for his allotted water bottle and took a swallow. He sorted through recent time. One day ago he had arrived in Sierra Madre. Two days ago he had been in New York getting his marching orders from Cath and Diana. Three days ago he had been raging and weeping on the beach at Provincetown. Four days ago he had been feeding the stupid Rhode Island Reds. Four days ago he had also fucked his wife in the open air with a pride and power that embarrassed him now. And five days ago had been the seventh anniversary of Ryan's death—and all those other deaths.

"Are you feeling okay, Mr. Wicklow, sir?" Lise asked from somewhere above him. She had put on a Red Cross sweatshirt. Had she been up all night?

"I just woke up." Jim felt like a kid talking to his mother. "I'm fine."

"If there's anything in Nina's backpack, could you let me know? If it tells us where she is, okay?"

"Sure," Jim said, covering a renewed alarm that emerged suddenly. He felt himself flailing with the realization that whatever intimacy had been established between them the day before had been put in reserve or lost altogether.

"Stay hydrated." Lise walked away.

Jim had dropped the barely-there backpack and his jacket under the cot. He swept his arm below to confirm they were still there. He couldn't face the contents of Nina's world just yet so he turned on his side and watched Lise move through the room. She seemed taller now and had to bend down to talk to the people who were lying in the cots. She helped an old man sit up. She put her hand on his wrist and looked at her watch for a while. Then Jim watched her gently prod at the man in a few places. She pulled a stethoscope from somewhere and listened to the old man's chest and back. Then she helped him lie down again before walking away.

Jim panicked. Why was she leaving this old man alone? He obviously needed help. Why was she walking away? Jim wanted to get up off the cot, run after her and drag her back to the old man. He wanted to stand over her while she cared for the old man, watching her heal him. But he lay where he was, willing his heartbeat to slow and his breathing to ease as he listened to the quiet early morning sounds of disasters, natural and manmade.

Later, after he left his cot, he sat at one of the tables, drank burnt coffee and went through the backpack. It was an unstructured thin nylon sack and the contents had barely any weight to them. When it hung on his shoulder it hardly felt like anything at all.

He unzipped all the zippers and ran his fingers inside all the pockets and deep nylon spaces. An empty crumpled Marlboro Lights soft pack with tobacco grains caught between the paper and the cellophane. A tube of Blistex with SPF 15. Several soft moist sections of the *Los Angeles Times* from September 8, 2008. A misshapen Luna bar. Paycheck stubs from a company name that revealed nothing about what she had done to earn the salary. A ten dollar bill and three ones. Endless pennies, nickels and dimes, as if she couldn't be bothered to count or care about coins, just tossing them into the backpack whenever they were handed to her. Several pieces of white maybe-cotton that felt like the soft flannel shirts J.J. used to wear. The fabric was stained with smears of what he guessed was machine grease. Jim thought of guys who worked on cars in their garages. The flannel pieces worried him because he couldn't decipher them and because he knew they came from the other world that all these wounded people had returned from. He would have to ask one of them about the grease and that worried him more.

In an interior pocket with no zipper Jim found a creased postcard of cherry blossom trees in Washington, D.C. It was addressed to Nina at Ryan's Brooklyn address and was postmarked on a smudged date in 1997. It read: *Daddy wishes you were here.* Jim couldn't remember why Ryan had been in D.C. Nina would have been ten, a ten-year-old getting a postcard from her dad from a city that seemed very far away and very beautiful. It had probably been an overnight trip.

Jim stared at the backpack's contents spread out on the table next to his coffee cup and torn packets of Splenda. His mind blanked from searching for too much meaning.

"I thought you were going to let me know if you found something."

Jim looked up at Lise sitting opposite him. He felt their connection again as if the earlier break had been something he had made up.

Jim gestured with both his hands, palms up, presenting the objects like a magician finishing a trick.

"Anything?" Lise didn't seem to want to look for herself.

Jim gingerly held up the pieces of smeared cloth by their edges. Lise stared with her flat dark eyes, her usual nothing face.

"Ask someone else."

He handed the postcard to Lise who took too long reading it. How damaged was her brain? Eventually she looked up, blank-faced, eyes darting, and handed the postcard back to him.

He watched Lise look over the other objects, determined not to stare too closely or touch any of them. She wouldn't look where he had laid the flannel things. She seemed to be attempting to count the coins, but moved on before she could possibly have finished. Her gaze hung over the smashed Luna bar and Jim wondered if she was hungry.

"Catch you later." And she was gone.

Slowly and with such care he thought fleetingly of an elderly relative he had visited once, Jim placed the items back into the backpack in the sections and pockets where he had found them. He took the tattoo sketches, the pill bottle, the drug patch and Nina's phone from his jacket pockets and placed them all in the backpack. Everything he had of Nina was now in one place. He re-zipped all the zippers, pressed closed all the pockets and slung the hardly-there backpack over his shoulder and went in search of his niece.

He found Nik.

Somewhere in the semi-sleep of the night before Jim had become determined to overcome his fear of Nik. Nik had answers. Nik could help him find Nina. So when he found him and the ever-present Acevedo and Maxwell getting into Nik's truck in the parking lot, Jim hailed Nik with as tough of a gesture as he could manage.

"Uncle Jim, you made it through," said Nik, one dusty brown boot in the door well, his surprisingly delicate hand resting on the open window frame of the truck.

"Can I ask you a few questions about Nina? Where she might be? Who she's with?" Jim blurted this, wanting to establish ground quickly.

"No good morning? No, did you make it through okay? How's the house?" Nik wasn't at full speed Nik-ness yet, but he was on his way. Jim could sense worry and it pleased him that he was able to read this guy, see what mattered to him.

"How's the house?" Jim offered.

Nik seemed to snap-to having gotten Jim to say the words he wanted. "We're going up there now to see. Come along."

Jim didn't hesitate. He walked around the front to the passenger side while Acevedo and Maxwell climbed into the empty bed of the truck—what had happened to that long box? There was a slow-motion moment when Jim met Nik's eyes behind the wheel, feeling in his rifle sights as he moved around the hood of the truck to the passenger side. Once inside Jim shoved himself into the door to be as far away as he could from Nik on the shared seat. He propped his elbow up on the edge of the open window.

The bright suburban streets quickly gave way to the hillside nooks and crannies of the lower canyon. When Nik made the turn onto the road to the upper canyon, Jim tried to keep breathing, watching Nik down shift as they climbed. The smell of smoke was heavy and large flakes of ash floated in the air. Jim cranked up the window using the handle, but the glass stopped half-way and the handle wouldn't turn anymore.

They crossed through a four-way stop without actually stopping and rose up onto a ridge. Jim swung his head from one side of the street to the other, seeing one intact house, then another, and then—disaster-scape.

Nik slammed on the brakes. Jim heard Acevedo and Maxwell bump and grumble behind him. There were houses and greenery and then there weren't. The demarcation line was an invisible divider between things and no things.

Jim's present-tense world sank in on him as he looked around. He had seen all this before. White-ish ash covered blackened melted shapes. There were empty places where he knew things had been before they were vaporized by heat and flame and collapse.

"Seventh house in," Nik said, easing the truck forward.

Jim silently counted molten structures until Nik pulled the truck into the drive of the seventh husk of a home. There was nothing to orient Jim, nothing to tell him he'd been in this place the day before. Fire could do this kind of damage this quickly and then just stop and retreat and leave room and time for people to return. He knew this.

Nik killed the engine and Acevedo and Maxwell jumped out of the truck bed. Jim and Nik sat staring through the dusty windshield, listening to the tinking of the truck in the hovering silence. People and animals had fled. The fire and firefighters were long gone and all that was left were the creaks and snaps of a broken world.

"Fuck me," Nik said.

"That would be about right," Jim responded, echoing Nik's taunt to him from the night before.

"Atta boy, Uncle Jim. Knew you were a street fighting man."

They walked the hissing landscape, Nik with purpose and inspection, Jim wandering in arcs around the wet and smoldering embers. Strange things survived, un-sooted and whole: a color photo, a dinner plate, a light bulb. Yes, he had seen this before, had run from it even as it coated him.

Jim looked up into the sky, blue but not bright. There were clouds and smears of smoke. The smoke stains reminded him that he wanted to ask Nik—or maybe Acevedo or Maxwell—about the greasy cloths in Nina's backpack. He looked around, didn't see Nik or the others, and looked back up into the sky. The silence was so heavy around him he wasn't sure if his transient deafness had returned. From that place in his brain where he kept all the television he had watched came the information he needed. The cotton cloths were used to clean guns. He knew this now. This knowledge triggered the same thoughts that had come to him days earlier on the beach at Provincetown. The sky pressing down on him, the buildings going down, taking him down, swirling whirling him to the ground. His knees swerved, but he remained standing, searching in the debris.

Jim had read later, or heard someone say it—or just simply absorbed the data as part of the lore of that day—that airline pilots had a name for that kind of weather: severe clear. The word "severe" had hung with him, occupying a narrow place in him that only had space for one word. There were mornings both in the city and on the Cape when he had inhaled the weather and light to compare them to that Tuesday morning, but it wasn't like ordering food in a restaurant when tastes could be summoned whenever he wanted to re-experience them. He almost passed out one morning, nearly hyperventilating, breathing in over and over trying to determine if a particular morning was like that other morning—no, lighter, darker, warmer, cooler, not quite.

Jim's brain physically shifted its parts. Something real and organic moved inside his head. This wasn't a memory or a dream, there had been a popping or a sliding of something within his skull, deep inside the brain, maybe where it was soft but definitely still material.

Sarah would tell him to buck up without actually saying it, refer to her tough father or just give him that look that told him he didn't deserve her or the other good things in his life if he was going to act this way. The evening they had married they helped each other dress. She was brushing the shoulders of his jacket when she told him she was sorry Ryan wasn't there to stand up for him. Jim had teetered slightly when Sarah said his name. "You must be thinking about him a lot today," Sarah said, but Jim hadn't thought of Ryan all day. But then he couldn't stop thinking about Ryan after she had said his name, opened the door, let that day come rushing into their evening. It had been the right thing to say—Sarah was always doing the right emotional thing for him—and the last thing he had wanted.

Here she was again as if via remote control. Clicking inside his head and reminding him to think about Ryan, face his absence. Here, among the charred ruins of a crazy guy's house. Jim felt smoke and ash cover him again in that way that only that day offered up.

He took the subway to work. He entered the building, he rode the elevator, he walked the hall, past the receptionist, past the open seating, into his office, back out toward the company kitchen—to get what? The thudding jolt, the sway of the building-scape around him, the idea of an earthquake formed in his mind. For a long time after, he and his colleagues experienced what he came to call fire-drill confusion. Do I really have to leave my work, it's just a drill, right? Seriously, because I have better things to do. What if it was the real thing? How could it be? Comfortable corporate confusion. But phones kept ringing—did they?—and the power went—or had it already?—and someone official said they should probably leave the building. Now. And then it was real, whatever it was—not the thing that had happened, which would never be real—real enough to mean he had to act, move, go now. *Daddy wishes you were here.*

And so they went down the stairs, in the dark, with grim uniformed faces passing them going up. Out on the street he felt stupid, like he was wasting his time, could be making money, but there were bad things happening around him and above him and he felt in the middle of something they were all sharing, just not sharing in exactly the same way. He was alone smelling what he smelled, seeing what he saw and feeling what he felt, and he was sure as he moved across the street that the people he passed were having an entirely different experience than the one he was having. They were smelling, seeing and feeling entirely different things even as they shared the same moment, the same space. The weather bound them all together, but even as the shouting and gesturing police told them to move fast move now, they were separate from each other, running away from the same falling engulfing ash force, propelled by their own separate fears and toward their separate havens.

As he waited for Cath to open her apartment door to him, he thought of Ryan for only the second time that morning. He stood, covered in white, cowering in a shamed way that barely registered, wondering why he hadn't thought more fully about where his brother was. Cath opened the door and Jim knew he better say something about their brother. For some reason he was absolutely sure that what he said was the truth, even though he made it up on the spot.

*Daddy wishes you were here.*

"Looking a little ashy, Uncle Jim." Nik interrupted, sneering his way into Jim's presence.

"Nina has a gun," Jim said.

## SIXTEEN

Lise wandered out of St. Rita's, finding her way along the streets of Sierra Madre to where she had parked the Jetta. She sat heavily in the driver's seat, the door open, her borrowed sneakers firmly planted on the black top. If she turned on the radio, she knew there would be a song playing that would blow her mind. It was like after she said goodbye to her dying grandfather, her mother standing shaken and stoic in the doorway, and getting in the Taurus and turning on the radio and hearing Blue Oyster Cult finishing "Don't Fear the Reaper." The universe was always giving Lise shit she didn't need. If she turned on the radio now, she was sure there would be more of *the warm smell of colitas.*

She wanted to close the car door, start the engine and drive somewhere, but she didn't know where to go. She should be following the clues in Nina's backpack, following Nina's trail, but the contents didn't offer a clear direction. And even if Lise caught up with Nina, what would she say to her, what would make it better?

Lise drove to the apartment she called home over Major Beck's garage.

She had climbed two steps of the outer stairs when Major Beck opened his back door.

"Captain, get your ass in here. There's baking going on." He gently issued the orders and then disappeared back into the kitchen, leaving the door open.

The kitchen smelled like cooking—baking dough, soft butter and grainy sugar—even though all the windows were open. The house held the smell but not the heat of whatever it was Major Beck was working on. Sauce pans were on three burners of the stove, there were different size bowls all over the kitchen. Spoons and things Lise thought were called whisks lay on counters, sticky with creamy smears. Both ovens were on at high temperatures and the refrigerator door was open, revealing stacks of butter sticks, cartons of milk and cardboard boxes of blue and red berries.

Major Beck, his back to her, stirred something in one of the pans on the stove. Lise stood still for a moment, identifying and ordering the kitchen world. The movement and chaos subsided into a tamed landscape and she listened to her own steady breathing, feeling her limbs, solid and useful.

"Can you mash those bananas for me, please? There's been a request for banana bread from my youngest for her birthday. I'll be in Baghdad so we've got to freeze a few loaves." Major Beck didn't turn when he spoke, continuing to perform mysterious activities at the stove.

Lise shifted her vision to the large butcher block kitchen table where a bunch of bananas sat next to a bowl and a steel utensil with a wood handle she knew was called a masher. She sat at the table, broke a banana off the stem and was half-through peeling it when she realized she knew how to do this.

Major Beck spun a narrative over Lise's head as she bowed into the bowl before her and concentrated on mashing the bananas. "Most of it's easy to make. I mean, seriously, fruit tarts? Made them a hundred times. Cream puffs are delicate, but you get the hang of it after a few years. The canelés on the other hand. First time last week, it's some big trend now. A pastry trend outside of France, who knew? Well, it is California. Fruit tarts, cream puffs and canelés—all before I get on the transport tomorrow. And the banana bread. How's the mashing coming, Captain?"

"Fine sir," Lise answered automatically, but pressed the masher more deliberately.

The next hour was like surgery at the Cash only it smelled bet-

ter. Lise stood at Major Beck's side, watching him, responding when
he asked her to hand him something, perform some task, spoon out
custard, grease a pan, set the timer. He asked for a spoon in the same
soft tones he asked for an amputation set. They cleaned up together,
washing and drying the bowls and utensils, wiping down the counter
tops and the stove, pushing crumbs and smears from the table with a
sponge into their cupped hands.

Lise sat at the table staring at the closed oven doors, imagining the transformative chemistry that was happening behind the black
enamel. Major Beck put a plate in front of her with a thick slice of
brown bread on it. Butter was spread evenly across the top. "Caffeine
or alcohol, Captain?" Lise looked up to see Major Beck standing by the
open fridge, the bottom shelf holding beer bottles and Coke cans. "Up
or down, Lise?"

"Down sir please." Lise stared at the bread, wondering how to
eat it, if she could move the bites through her throat.

Major Beck put an uncapped bottle of Sierra Nevada next to her
plate. He sat opposite her at the table, eating his buttered slice of bread
and sipping at a can of diet Coke.

"Did you find Nina?"

"We found her backpack. She left it behind." Lise took a bite of
the bread so she wouldn't have to say another word for the few moments it would take to chew and swallow.

"She went off with this guy then? On a bender?" Major Beck
talked with his mouth full.

"She's been having a hard time."

"Who hasn't?"

Lise looked at Major Beck, examining the crooked part in his
new haircut, the stained Van Halen T-shirt, the line of his farmer's tan
sneaking out of the sleeves and neck. One set of his surgeon's fingers
were gracefully wrapped around the soda can, the other pinched his
half-eaten bread slice. This was the man who calmed them in the Cash,
set their course with confidence. *Know you're doing the right thing.*

"She's not okay, is she?" Lise asked, mostly to make conversation.

"No one is."

"But I still have to find her. That's what I have to do."

"That's what you have to do."

"And?"

Major Beck didn't say anything.

"This never goes away," she said, more to herself than to him. Lise thought another person would get teary-eyed, something in the throat, a clenched face—something, anything. Nothing.

Major Beck stared at her and Lise wondered if there was a telepathic message she should be receiving. She remembered Major Beck's connection to Nina's landlady—his child in school with Mia, knowing Jen. Then she thought of Jim and Danny and the sniper and the hard-bodied guy with the tattooed vines on his arms. There was a crowd of people in her head.

"The little girl, the landlady's daughter—Mia, the one you know."

Major Beck smiled a small snort of recognition. "She's a cutey."

"She wears a bow-and-arrow thing on her back, a basket-thing for arrows."

"I think it's called a quiver." He wasn't smiling now.

"Yeah, a quiver." Lise liked the word, it felt like a right word, not something she had gotten wrong. "Anyway, she wears a toy one from some warrior princess cartoon strapped to her back, with plastic arrows and a bow stuck in it. I think she sleeps with it on, or wants to anyway."

"Don't we all." Major Beck got up from the table and put his plate in the sink. "Lise, listen. Get something else going on, something that'll put it back together for you."

"But not them," Lise said quickly. "It doesn't put them back together."

"No, just us."

## SEVENTEEN

Jen woke on the couch, her back to the room. She could feel that it wasn't quite morning yet as she stared at the fabric of the upholstery. She knew Marco sat in a chair nearby, staring at her shoulders, willing her to wake before Mia did.

She rolled onto her back, closed her eyes and tried to make her husband go away. She raised her forearms and laid them across the bridge of her nose. This did not ward off what was coming.

"One hundred twenty four thousand, eight hundred fifty six and change," Marco said, slowly, keeping his voice high, his tone loose. No judgment. "Plus the mortgages and what we owe on the cars."

Jen thought about finding something to say in response, but she got lost in the maze of language available.

"I've been learning all kinds of new words, reading," said Marco. "We're what's called upside down on the condo. If we can manage to sell it, it will be this thing called a short sale. This place and the rental and the other house on Mira Monte—we'll get money, if there's anyone who wants to buy them, who can buy them. We won't make a profit from them, but we'll have cash in hand to pay off the credit cards. One hundred twenty four thousand, eight hundred fifty six and change."

Jen knew the number, had always known the number even as it changed, adding digits over the years—but she had managed to believe it didn't really belong to her.

"The new words are kind of interesting if you don't stop to think about what they mean in actual real life," Marco said. The new words were not interesting, but Jen was on board with not thinking about what they meant.

"We'll have a cushion when we're done and we'll need a low monthly nut. We won't have the cars, gas. Mia's school will cost more. The house payments versus rent will likely be a wash, but maybe we can find a deal when we get there. Maybe we can even own again, whatever that means." All of this jarred Jen and she finally spoke, enunciating beyond her forearms, still laid across her face.

"Get where?"

"We're moving back to Brooklyn."

She pulled her hands down and sat up almost in one motion to confront him, her sneakers landing on the floor, reminding her she had slept with them on. She lifted her eyes slowly to face him.

When Marco had uttered the word California back in the middle of her New York nightmare, she had found relief and excitement in the healing suggestion of moving, changing their lives, fixing everything. But now, this same effort in reverse caused her alarm. They had come here to restore themselves to each other. They had failed, but going back to Brooklyn felt like a worse defeat. She would be waiting for him as he assessed when the right time would be to announce they were divorcing; no there wasn't anyone else, there was just no more of this.

"I can't hold this in my head. It just won't hold." She felt her brain softening even as she said this, readying itself to learn the new words, calculate the new math. "New York's expensive so how is it an option?"

"Expensive depends on how you live. We need a different default position. Some of our givens need to change."

"What are our givens now?"

"I love you and you can't feel it. And Mia—she's a given. And we think we need to spend a lot of money."

This was Marco at his best, and why she never really believed she would die even when she thought she was dead already. He was trying to get down to basics, but she still wanted to resist.

"Won't we think we need to spend a lot of money in Brooklyn? Isn't that how you live there, anywhere? This life is expensive."

"Yes, it is."

"That's not some kind of California hippie shit double meaning, is it?"

"The New Yorker cornered," he shot back.

Jen went down to her knees, collapsing her upper body over her thighs, fists landing on the rug under her, crumbling before Marco the way others pray, bodies prone, facing Mecca. Jen emptied herself out through tears, crying that began gently and sustained even as he joined her on the floor, trying to pull her body into the comfort of his.

He continued his new custom of urgently muttering into the hair matted on her cheek. "Remember what it was like before? We'd go out, you were funny and weird, and—and it was just…" Marco's lips stopped moving on her skin.

Jen realized the word he was going to say. Their life had been *good*. What was it now?

"Bottom line is we need to earn wherever we live. We need to make money. We can't make money here. There're no jobs for you at all and I'm just another guy, tons of kids who do what I do and no one here cares they're kids who eat their boogers."

Something fell loose in her and she chuckled deep inside, thinking of the sleeping Mia's fondness for flicking her tongue at the mucus from her nose, but Jen pushed the momentary lightness down under the oppressive horror of what she was being forced to confront.

"Jen, baby, listen to me. There's no work here and we've gotten into this bad habit of spending money we don't have. There'll be work in New York, even with this crash thing. There're sick-money jobs—jobs that take your soul—but sick-money like you get nowhere else on earth."

She pulled away from him, pressed the hair and tears away from her face, inhaled deeply through her clogged nose. "But the sick-money kills us. How will we get better?"

"We'll save it and when we spend it, we'll spend it differently."

"I don't know what that means. I don't know what that is."

"We'll get there."

"I can't see it. I don't believe it's there."

"You can do it. You can walk into an agency and score some sick-paying group account director gig and you'll give them fifty hours a week and you'll come home to Mia and me and you'll be okay. I'll do some tech director thing at a straight place that thinks I'm the shit because I'm not twelve and I clean up well. We don't have to believe, we just have to get paid."

"What do I believe in then?"

Marco looked at her like she had just asked for a cocktail, seconds after agreeing to go to rehab. Then Mia shuffled into the room in her green turtle slippers.

"I'm still sleepy, but I want cereal now, please," Mia announced.

Later, they did the math together, at the kitchen table, papers spread out around Mia and her breakfast, pens scratching, fingers poking at the calculator on the new phone's touch screen.

The things they had bought, the life they had assembled. So much stuff.

"This feels like strip poker and I'm losing," Jen said, holding the last three monthly statements for one of the Visa cards. "And I haven't shaved my underarms or waxed my bikini. But other than that, this counting our chickens feels awesome." The New York sass didn't sound right to her ears. She wasn't going to be able to make this work.

"Don't make me laugh. It's the end of the world," Marco said.

"Can I have a bikini, Mommy?" Mia asked. She tilted the cereal bowl to her mouth and loudly slurped up the remnant milk.

Jen stared at her daughter as she violated much-repeated rules about utensils and eating noises. Was this a conscious test? Did the

child grasp that all regulations had been suspended while Mommy
and Daddy got their shit together?

"So we're going to get gangsta? That's it? This is how we get
out of debt?" Jen looked from Mia to her husband, hoping for a
normalizing response from him.

"Don't push the smiley funny stuff because you're still half-
way the depressed junkie bitch." Marco dropped his voice to a harsh
whisper. "Who spent six hundred dollars on a cashmere T-shirt she
wore once just so she could feel good for two minutes." He cut a
look at Mia before leveling a stare at Jen.

Jen saw Mia's eyes go wide at the word that made Mom-
my mad, but Mia stayed silent, soft lashes fluttering rapidly as she
blinked away the sounds of her parents.

Jen had nothing to say. She stared at the numbers in front of
her, turning away from her husband and her child. Her mood fell,
descending beneath the gallows humor she had embraced for the
last hour. Some intolerable changes were still in the offing and she
was the source of all that had been wrecked and needed repair. She
would have to be the source too of all this awful change.

Marco laid out the sets of keys from all the properties and all
the vehicles next to Mia's crusting glass of orange juice. Jen stared
at the different color metals, the rings, the logos and address tags.

"I can't find the keys to Palm Desert," Marco said.

"We left them in the drawer of that thing in the front hall.
Didn't we?" Jen was surprised at what she remembered and what
she didn't.

"Nina went to the desert," Mia said quietly, intent on her
spoon, scraping at the bottom of the empty bowl.

"Nina?" Jen knew what she was going to hear.

"She took the keys. After she gave me the bow and arrows."
Mia looked at Marco. "Is she mad about Nina's present?"

"Mommy's not mad," Marco said to Mia, looking at Jen.

Jen tried to telepathically communicate with Marco. It wasn't
that she didn't want Mia to hear, it was that she couldn't form the
words out loud.

"You're going to have to say it. If you're walking out that door, you need to say it," Marco said.

"She's missing."

"I thought you were getting back on board."

Mia put both her hands in her lap and Jen obeyed her daughter's unspoken command. She put her hand on Marco's thigh and he immediately covered it with both of his.

"Just a few hours and then I'm back," Jen promised.

## EIGHTEEN

Danny Gold opened his eyes: FADE IN.

People—young, old, families, a dog or two—milled throughout St. Rita's. Some lay on cots or sat in huddles at the TVs, craning their necks to receive the information stream. Danny could almost see the words and numbers flowing in the air. The CGI would make them glow electronic green as they danced through the air. Volunteers—amateur and professional, some in identifying T-shirts and jackets—moved from group to group, offering help of all kinds. There was paper work, introductions to insurance company reps and FEMA and the SBA. The FEMA guys, with their expressions of pain-under-the-cheer, looked like they were sick of explaining themselves. The fire department wanted to know if firefighters would be safe on people's property when they got there. CLOSE-UP: faces colored with fear, excitement, worry, impatience, anticipation, boredom. Starbucks had donated coffee, and full *venti*-size paper cups sat under cots, logos visible. People wanted to sleep, relax, disconnect from the jitters of evacuee life—not drink lattes.

He followed Lise, tracking behind her as she moved through St. Rita's from person to person. ZOOM IN: on the people she spoke with. But the cuts felt cheesy so he panned off to a jittery hand-held shot when the action required it. If he could capture it on paper, the camera would love her, so informed and efficient, touching people, talking to them, doing things that people did when they wore uniforms. By dawn he couldn't keep up with her, could barely stay awake.

He walked through the residential streets of Sierra Madre in that first warming light of the day—the stench of burning still in the air—and stopped on a corner near Nina's house. He forgot for a moment where he'd parked his car. It took him some time to find it.

He sat in the car, fighting sleep, and went over his notes, feeling slightly overwhelmed by everything he had written and panicking when he couldn't read his scribbles. He tried not to think of how scared he was. He'd deal with Lise's weird world because he was going to write the hell out of it. He wasn't sure what it was—a parallel storyline for the Iraq story he'd been working on with her or maybe something entirely separate. It felt big—agent-shrieking-big. A high-six payday, easy.

Nik flipped Danny out completely, but Danny could see him in a cartoon as Sixties Dude which neutralized his threat. Nik also reminded him of every egomaniacal creative director at the ad agency he'd worked at back in New York and every movie director he'd met since he'd been in L.A. They were all a potent mix of crazy and bullshit with a dash of calculating thrown in. Great material, Dennis Hopper dialogue, though he'd heard Hopper had some kind of bad cancer.

He was equally cowed by Jim. It wasn't fear, more concern that he'd been found out. What if East Coast Jim was here to stop Danny's West Coast reinvention and drag him back to his New York days when he was just another schmuck in advertising? He'd run five years before from his New York copywriter existence and he wanted to wipe it from the face of the earth. He had handled Jim, he hoped, with some half-ass posturing he'd picked up watching actors pretending not to be recognized at Trader Joe's and Sushi Roku. He'd even borrowed a line from a movie he prayed Jim hadn't seen.

Danny finally started the car and headed out of Sierra Madre. He hit traffic on his way along the mountains and down into Studio City. The AC brought air in from the outside. He had never been able figure out how to switch it to internal recycled air so he smelled smoke all the way home. He thought for a split second about taking a shower after he got through his door, but instead turned on the television and sprawled on the bed.

The TV screamed at him about the collapse of the invisible engine that drives American life. It was the biggest disaster movie of the year except no one could possibly make the dialogue both authentic and understandable to the average moviegoer. It was too big to explain. Maybe it was *Star Trek*, a morality play about what we can't understand but want to destroy.

The TV told him the wildfire that had spread through the Angeles National Forest and burned in the hills north of Sierra Madre would be officially contained by early afternoon. Fires were still burning farther north and south near San Diego. The government had bailed out AIG and the stock market was up a little. Danny tried to absorb the conversations that aligned this new information with yesterday's failure of Lehman and the steep drop of the market. Up and down, was all he thought. Or, down and up, depending on where you had come in. He turned off the TV, feigned sleep for a few moments, then returned to the action at St. Rita's.

FADE IN: ST. RITA'S BASEMENT – RED CROSS COTS – DAY.

Danny pressed his shoulders against the wall and widened his eyes. He framed the scene, focused his internal lens. What's interesting? It was all interesting. He closed his eyes—too much information—sat down on the floor, his back against the wall. His legs stretched out in front of him and the laptop rested on his thighs. He realized he'd forgotten the power cord at home and his battery was at eighty-two percent and draining fast. He was afraid if he returned home for the power cord he'd miss out on so much. He'd just have to write fast.

Of course, the scene around him held echoes of New York on September 11th, but the blackout in the city two years later was the stronger memory for Danny. Maybe he'd been too freaked out in 2001 to absorb images—too scared and drunk, too lost between the legs of a new girlfriend. But during that power outage—total northeastern grid failure, if he remembered right—once the sheer terror of nine-eleven playback had subsided, the blackout of 2003 provided absolute clarity of memory for him.

A gorgeous New York City August afternoon and the power went. If it hadn't been for the air conditioning and office computers going down, the loss of light would have gone unnoticed. New Yorkers, Danny included, were so relieved they weren't being bombed—that they were going to live—that they gathered in the streets, on stoops, by the rivers, in parks, sharing bottles and joy. The city darkened and the gentle parties continued, the new friends around him offering company until morning when power returned. The clusters of people in the rooms here at St. Rita's reminded him of that tender city night. And as evenly tempered as that day-night had been, it was the event that ultimately brought urgency to his escape from New York. He was living in Los Angeles by Christmas of that year, running from a kind of claustrophobia.

Danny focused on the screen in front of him, willing the cursor to blink. He gave up, closed the laptop and went looking for Lise.

He walked into the room the Red Cross had set up as a cafeteria. He scanned the room, panning left to right. He saw Jim sitting at a table, not eating the food in front of him, fiddling with a zipper on what he knew to be Nina's backpack. He focused on him for a moment then panned away. He initially wanted to avoid Jim, but thought better of it, moved toward him and joined him at the table.

"Hey." Danny kept things terse. He figured the less he said, the tougher he seemed.

Jim looked at Danny and took a sip from a diet Coke can.

"Hey," Jim responded in kind.

"Some fire, huh?" Danny immediately regretted this inanity.

"Went up with Nik to see his place." Jim seemed to be boasting.

"And?"

"Gone."

Danny wanted to ask him to describe the scene, but didn't. He opened his laptop and placed it between the two of them on the table. His battery had somehow become more depleted in Sleep mode. Fuck Apple. He swiveled his head back and forth from Jim to the screen and typed random thoughts and scene ideas mostly just to relieve the tension in his hands.

"You writing a screenplay or something?"

"Just taking some notes, trying to order what's happening."

"Good luck with that."

"I'll make most of it up. These notes'll just help with my memory." Danny felt stupid with this half-ass attempt to explain how he worked. He got stuff right and he met his deadlines—what else mattered?

He wandered away from Jim, through rooms and hallways, his laptop folded under his arm, held to his chest. No one looked familiar. He wondered where Lise was, and Maxwell and Acevedo and Nik.

He heard their voices before he could place them. He followed their off-camera dialogue down a hallway until he came to an office. They were all assembled for what he assumed was a regularly scheduled group therapy session. Montage idea: quick cuts across a series of meetings, funny and sad dialogue contrasted. He needed to hear their speech rhythms so he lurked in the doorway and hoped they wouldn't notice him.

Nik sat on top of a desk. Maxwell and Acevedo had pulled up chairs to face Nik and a pimply pale boy-man Danny had never seen before stood leaning against a file cabinet. Lise sat on an office chair with a crooked back rest. She faced Nik with her back to the doorway. Danny stood behind her, staring at her shoulders.

"You need like three showers man," Maxwell said to Acevedo.

"Sorry I can't smell all sweet and spicy like you," Acevedo shot back.

"Bunch a girls you got here," said the pimply pale kid.

"Not that there's anything wrong with girls right Sheridan?"

Acevedo smiled weakly at Lise.

"Oh we like girls and girls dig war heroes and medals and guns and money," chimed Maxwell.

"We like the honeys who like money." The men were into their back-and-forth rhythm now.

"Honeys definitely dig money wouldn't be patriotic if the ladies didn't dig the money not that you got any of that money with your government direct deposit to your mommy's bank account." Maxwell kept looking at Lise, checking to see if he was impressing or insulting her.

"I am so looking forward to not seeing you guys for a while." Acevedo looked around the room, failed to notice Danny, much to Danny's relief.

"You'll get your robo-arm man it's been all fixed up for you." Maxwell slapped Acevedo's thigh. "VA's going to get that thing right this time a few weeks of cush rehab and you're back here kicking my ass in *Call of Duty* all hands on deck." There was more laughter than Danny thought cool about an amputee's prosthesis. He retreated a step into the hallway just to turn down the volume.

"I can go active duty again once they get the robo-arm right back with the unit." Acevedo looked at the floor as he spoke.

This seemed to be a good thing since they all fell silent, bowing their heads to this possibility.

Acevedo looked to the pale kid and said, "Dude I'll never forget you coming out of the sky on that whirly-bird screaming like your hair was on fire rushing that stretcher to us."

"Like a fairy god-medic on that Black Hawk coming down from the medevac clouds," Maxwell added.

Danny skimmed through a series of images from various movies of dusty village touchdowns by helicopters in numerous parts of the world. He saw crouched soldiers hustling stretchers filled with wounded to a chopper. Huddling under the rapidly spinning blades they loaded their buddies and slapped the sides of the machine's doors in benedictions for safe travel. The heavy metal soundtrack obliterated the slow whomp-whomp of the in-scene sounds.

"And you had your tourniquet pulled tight and a fentanyl lollipop in his mouth," Pale Kid said to Maxwell.

"You did good Doc." Acevedo told Maxwell, likely for the hundredth time.

"Wished I'd pulled that tourniquet better fucking haji IED."

"One arm made it Doc when and where it counted." Acevedo reached out his good arm. Danny thought he should maybe tap at the keyboard, get these details down, but he was frozen, listening, waiting for Lise to say something.

Danny wondered what she was thinking, what the expression on her face might be. Her shoulders were lifted almost to her ears as if she was bracing for something. He wasn't even sure she was inhaling and exhaling. Suddenly Acevedo looked straight at Lise. For a second Danny thought he was looking beyond her to him, but then Acevedo reached out his only hand to Lise.

"Chain of care true?" Acevedo looked to Lise.

"True but we took your arm in the Cash," Lise said, loud and clear for everyone to hear. Still in the doorway, Danny was shocked by the sound of her voice. She sounded as if she had just learned to speak.

"Iraq took my arm Cash saved my life." Acevedo lowered his arm. Lise hadn't taken his hand.

Danny wondered if Lise had actually touched Acevedo's gone-arm, maybe even helped a surgeon cut away the dangling damaged limb.

Maxwell put his hand on Acevedo's empty shoulder and Pale Kid grabbed Maxwell's upper arm with his hand. The physical contact among the damaged startled Danny. He cringed like when he saw blind men tapping along the sidewalk when he was a kid.

Nik breathed deeply from on high, sitting cross-legged on the desk.

The four soldiers leaned toward each other, almost forming a circle in front of Nik. Danny watched Lise among these men, one of them but apart. He pulled back from the scene in his mind, craning up high over the leaning people as music from somewhere far away seeped in, offering a soundtrack. He let his eyes slowly soften, envisioning how the images would fade to black and the closing credits would crawl up the screen.

The mood broke as if they were actors breaking character after a director had yelled "cut." The men laughed, they reached for soda cans and moved their chairs. Nik uncrossed his legs. Only Lise seemed still altered, remaining in the other, intense world. She stood, turned and faced Danny. He wasn't sure she saw him.

Lise looked terrible, her skin slick with light grey sweat. She moved toward Danny, not really walking but somehow advancing across the floor. She pushed him back without touching him as she moved through the doorway and into the hallway. As she went past, he heard her whisper, "I can't breathe."

And then she was falling a little, her body sagging above the knees, her sneakers stuck in place. The wall broke her fall and she slid against it, half collapsed. Danny was too late to catch her and he was worried about the laptop in his arms, but he was able to break her further descent even as she righted herself against the wall. They leaned there together, awkwardly entangled, as Danny tried to hold both his laptop and Lise, and Lise supported herself with her own failing strength.

"Something bad," Lise said, only to herself.

Danny responded, "You're okay."

"Something's coming." She melted farther down the wall, through his arms and legs. He extracted the laptop from between them and placed it on the floor at his feet, quickly righting himself so their faces were close.

"You're okay," he said.

"It's bad."

He searched for things to say, smarter dialogue from better movies.

"It's coming," she insisted.

"It's over."

"Yeah?" Lise didn't seem to know whether or not to buy this. "Really?"

"Yeah, come and gone." He'd hit on something that worked

for her. "It's after."

"But I'm still here."

"You're still here."

Danny realized Nik was standing by them and he looked into Nik's dented face. Nik had nothing there for him, offering up another version of Lise's shallow eyes.

Danny shifted his focus into the deep field of vision down the corridor before him. He could see the entire cast. Jim reached out a hand to Jen who entered the scene, hitting her mark beside him. Marco stood behind her, tall and lean in the background. Mia sat on Marco's shoulders, towering over the crowd, her plastic arrows bobbing in the light framing her shoulders. Jim placed his fingers gently in the folds of Jen's shirt along her arm as if he was trying to get her attention. Mia reached down and softly patted her mother's hair. Danny pulled back wide, panning away from this distant intimacy, tracking back down the corridor and executing a smooth turn and tilt-up, past Maxwell and Acevedo, past Nik's unmoving face, settling back on Lise—her eyes wide and unblinking beneath the hair that fell across her cheeks.

"We're all still here," Danny said.

# PALM DESERT

# NINETEEN

Jen was determined to do the driving. She didn't care whose car they took, but there was no way slightly-drunk-definitely-not-paying-attention Lise was getting behind the wheel of a car. Nik—the Vietnam vet from the canyon—had tried to manage the negotiations over who was going to Palm Desert, who was driving, who would sit in which car, but in the end, after the shouting, he drifted out of St. Rita's parking lot, walking away with menacing murmurs, repeating "hey man." Once the others—Acevedo and Maxwell and the pale kid—had trailed after their damaged leader, it was left to Marco to say he would stay home with Mia. Jen looked at her three passengers—Danny, Lise and Jim—and thought *what the fuck.*

Jen had second and third thoughts and wanted a stop back at the house to make sure all was well with what she was leaving behind—just for a few hours down and back, not for good. Marco and Mia needed to be clear about that. Jen needed to be clear about that.

Marco was fine, in fact he kept acting as if it was his idea. He said she had to see these things for herself and that's how she would really get it.

"See Nina? What?" Jen's head hurt.

"Condo-land. These United States of Golf, this endless, pointless, deficit-financed shit," Marco said. Jen heard his anger, but was pretty sure Mia was stifling a giggle.

"We don't play golf," Jen offered feebly.

"Yeah right," was Marco's weird reply. In the last few hours his tone had veered into terrain she couldn't name. He was either coping or prepping—she couldn't figure out which. Jen worried about how Mia would be when she got back from the desert. "Can you do the daddy thing while I'm gone?" she asked him. "I'll be back tonight."

Marco seemed to snap into place like a puzzle piece, coming to attention and resting his hand on Mia's shoulder. "We'll stand guard on the home front."

"We'll keep you safe while you're gone," Mia said, indicating her bow and arrows.

Jen had made her decision and should have been fueled forward, but instead she idled in place. Her purse hung on her shoulder, her empty wallet with the maxed-out cards inside, the car keys in her hand. She couldn't get going.

Marco extracted old twenties from his wallet and folded them into her hand. "Gas money, babe. Drive safe."

When would he stop reading her mind?

When Jen got back to the car, Jim stared hard at her. "Let's just do what we need to do and get there." He was antsy, bouncing on the balls of his feet, probably realizing how much time he'd wasted. "Are we going?"

Lise and Danny conspired by the rear of the car, ready to react if Jen said the wrong thing.

"Get in. Let's go," Jen said, realizing Jim would end up in the passenger seat beside her. As they got into their seats, she sensed a raised eyebrow from Danny. He was also thinking about Jen and Jim sitting next to each other.

As she was speeding onto 210 East, Jim asked her if she was okay to drive.

She signaled to move into the center lane and the speedometer bobbed over seventy-five. "I'm good," she told him. "Less than two hours, Jim. We'll find her."

It was the first time she had said his name out loud. As soon as the sound fled her lips she realized with absolute assurance that they had known each other in some intimate way in the past. And she could see out of the corner of her eye that he looked like a man who suddenly knew this too. Quietly, more to sustain the fragile connection than to keep it from Lise and Danny, she said, "It's okay. It was a long time ago."

Marco had introduced Jen to this part of the world. She had never been to a desert before. When they first moved West, they left Mia with his parents and he took her out to Twentynine Palms. Her body operated differently, as did her brain. She and Marco experienced their connection in an altered, deeper way. They seemed restored to a natural state—stripped and improved. Maybe they were Adam and Eve before the Fall, wandering hand in hand among the cacti—or something like that. Maybe it was just what other people called "getting away from it all." She wondered if this desert world would have the same effect on her passengers. Jen turned on the radio to help their transition.

Jim sat large in his seat, awkwardly holding his knees together with his hands. He shot a look at Jen when he realized they were listening to lefty radio chronicling the fall of capitalism.

"They're all saying the same thing," she said. "There're no sides today."

Jim exhaled in response, put an elbow on the door's arm rest and turned his other hand into a fist. Lise checked the rearview and caught portions of Lise and Danny's heads.

As the sun set in the West behind them, Jen felt them all glow with the end of the day. Danny was alive in the seat right behind her and she could sense even Lise rising to room temperature as the desert sunset worked its magic. Jim shape-shifted next to her, one moment a partner in crime, the next a stranger she had picked up in exchange for a fare. The green destination signs along the side of the interstate guided them. Danny asked a question Jen couldn't catch, but she heard the uplift at the end of what he said and knew there was an answer pending from someone.

"What was that, Danny?" Jen spoke into the rearview mirror, flicking her eyes to the backseat. She reached down and lowered the volume of the radio chat.

"Those outlet malls are up here somewhere?"

Jen opened her mouth and then closed it again, feeling like a much-watched guppy in some kid's aquarium. She glanced over at Jim, who seemed to have settled into a waking coma with his eyes open. He likely hadn't heard Danny at all. Lise was a non-presence now, shut down in the back seat.

"Maybe on the way back? What do you think?" Jen said to the windshield, hoping the words would bounce to Danny. Was he really thinking about shopping? Her thoughts drifted from their task. The burden of being the driver descended on her. She had taken on too much, needed to stop pushing them all forward.

"We need gas," Jen said, although they didn't. She glanced at Jim, wondering if he would look at the fuel gauge. He was in a trance.

When they pulled into the station, Danny bolted from the car and disappeared into the store. Jen went through the motions of filling the tank, standing guard over the nozzle after she inserted it into the car. She could see Jim and Lise sitting motionless. The late afternoon desert removed air and time, suspending Jen in limbo until the gas nozzle flipped off with a jerk. She wasn't ready to get back in the driver's seat. Maybe she could just stand there a while longer. How many minutes would pass before Danny came out of the store or Lise or Jim got out of the car, wondering what was taking so long. How long could she delay?

"You want some?" Danny offered her a bottle of water.

She waved him off.

Lise got out of the car, barely acknowledged Danny and walked into the store. Jen feared for someone's safety—Lise's maybe or the people in the store—and moved swiftly after her.

The store was cool and antiseptic and empty. The cashier was another student, buried in a book, oblivious to the threats and transactions around him.

Jen found Lise drinking a beer, holding open one of the glass doors of the cold case. Jen watched her take large swallows of Tecate, thinking it must taste like the tin can it was in.

"Do you want some chips? I have some cash," Jen said, remembering the twenties Marco had pressed on her.

Lise said nothing, raising the beer. Jen wasn't sure if Lise was toasting her or offering her a sip.

Jen went to the cashier with a box of cookies she knew she wouldn't eat.

"My friend's drinking a beer back there," she said to the cashier. "Maybe two. How much is that?"

"He can't do that," the kid said, looking up from his book.

"He's a she and she's not driving," Jen said, finding some authority.

"Still, not cool." The kid asked which brand and size.

Jen handed over one of Marco's twenties.

Once they were outside in the cooling desert air, Lise said thank you.

"For the beers. And for driving."

Jen turned away and lifted her shirt so Lise could see the Milky Way bar shoved in her back pocket. She looked into Lise's eyes and found the shallow blackness that was always there.

"We should probably go now," Lise said.

Jen followed her to the car. Someone had put the gas hose away. She opened the little door to the fuel tank to check if the cap has been put back on properly. *Righty tighty lefty loosey.* She pulled her fingers away knowing they smelled of gas. There were no more delays to construct, no more detours. She had to drive.

The highway curved and dropped, descending into the San Gorgonio Pass between the two mountain ranges. In the graying near distance, the wind farm beckoned and pulled them in. They were about thirty miles from Palm Desert. Jen felt them all entering a weird world of vanishing light, but she could still see the tall white windmills whirring their blades in the air, looking like long-limbed, small-headed aliens from where? Not Mars, but maybe Neptune or Pluto. There were thousands of them, an army of 150-foot-tall space soldiers, spinning, pulling her—all of them—into their spindly white arms.

Night pressed in on them from all sides now as the day finally ended. Jen turned the parking lights to full brightness. The dashboard lit up with blue aviation glow. The NPR station had disappeared into static long ago. The exit sign for Palm Desert hovered and Jen lifted the turn signal with her finger. The white letters glowed on the green sign. The blinker's repeating click set the pace.

"Almost there," she said, looking at Jim as she pushed down on the brake, coming off the exit to a stop.

Jen's passengers came alive. Lise coughed like a motor starting and sat up straight, a clear presence now. Danny leaned forward and put his hand on the top of the driver's seat. Jim shifted in his seat and powered down the window. "Could you turn off the AC?"

"Yeah, let's smell that clean air." This, oddly, came from Lise, but it was robotic as if she had overheard someone else say it once, maybe in a movie.

Jen looked around, lowering her window to get a better look at the streets. "I think I took the first exit instead of the second. I need to get my bearings." Lise made a turn and they all looked around for landmarks in the unfamiliar landscape.

They passed Gerald Ford Drive and then Frank Sinatra Drive and Jen realized Marco was right: what had they been thinking? Why try to beat a real estate market? Why not just live?

Even as Jen found her way among the street signs and country club entrances, she worried about how they would get out of there. She wasn't sure she would be able to reverse her path back to the 10 or to Sierra Madre or to Brooklyn. Marco suddenly saw this all as constructed fake shit, waste—greenery and climate control in a no-water world. Desert lawns, for fuck's sake—why hadn't she seen it?

The entrance for the Oasis Country Club appeared on Jen's right. She made the turn and slowed as she passed the guard house, but no one was on duty. She sped up into the complex.

"Morocco Road, guys," Jen said.

"You're kidding," Danny answered.

And then they were there. Jen turned off the car, the four of them sat staring at the dark condo in front of them, small among the surrounding lighted homes.

The front door was not quite closed. Jen wondered if Jim saw it too. She felt a rush of confused feelings—it was good the door was open because she didn't have the key but she wouldn't need the key if Nina was there to let them in but doors that stood ajar seemed ominous. This helpful errand of driving Jim to find Nina had seemed urgent and necessary for Jen when they were still in Sierra Madre. Now, staring at the slightly open door, Jen experienced the rising dread of another ordeal she might be responsible for.

The four of them emerged in slow motion from the car. They closed their doors in an unintended syncopation that they all ignored. They walked—not with purpose but in the same direction, not as one but together—up the path between the miniature cactus landscaping and the soft green grass of the lawn.

Jim passed Jen just before they got to the door. Nina's backpack hung from one of his shoulders. Lise surged ahead, extending an arm in a too-late gesture of protection.

# TWENTY

Jim had a kind of inverted tunnel vision. He could see only what surrounded a dark spot right in the center of his vision. He was completely blind to what he was staring straight at.

He swung his head from side to side only dimly aware that there were people standing behind him. He knew Lise had his back and Jen was somewhere behind his left shoulder. He assumed Danny had not come inside. The three of them moved as one, stepping where the other stepped, cautiously, infused with anxiety as if moving through a minefield.

The open kitchen and eating area were to Jim's left and he drifted toward that part of the large space. A small light shone under the hood over the stove. There were dirty dishes in the sink, stacked as if they were about to fall. There were six packs of beer, a few bottles nesting in a divided cardboard case but more missing. Empty and full bottles of vodka and whiskey stood on the counter. Wet glasses had been used to put out cigarettes. The smell of moist ash threatened to gag Jim. He held his breath and moved on.

The large room had floor-to-ceiling windows and sliding doors all along the wall that fronted the golf course. With almost no light on in the condo, Jim could see through the glare of the glass to the lit-up homes and the busy country club night beyond. He moved along the windowed wall, picking up Jen and Lise's reflections in his peripheral vision.

There were overstuffed chairs and couches in the living room, and coffee table books on topics only Southern Californians could possibly care about. There were more empty bottles and sodden cigarette butts. He caught the glint of a torn paper packet with a slight metallic sheen. The image of the condom wrapper formed itself around his blind spot and it soothed him momentarily in a way he couldn't immediately register.

Jim made his way down the corridor to the bedrooms. He paused outside the first bedroom door. It was slightly ajar in the way the front door had been and it offered up the same tight anxiety for him. He paused his breathing as he pushed the door open with his fingertips.

He felt a presence behind him, probably Lise, slide a hand along the wall and turn on the overhead light.

He walked into the room and stood at the foot of the queen-size bed. His deafness returned, its comings and goings now revealing a purpose: his body was protecting him. He heard nothing and he saw without seeing.

Then his vision restored itself, the center blackness evaporating like steam clearing off a mirror.

There she was. Nina, found. There was a man beside her. Jim could see they weren't alive.

They were sitting up on the bed like a married couple reading before turning in for the night. They were leaning back against layers of pillows, cushioning them from the headboard of the bed. Jim couldn't look at Nina so he turned his strained eyes to the soldier beside her.

He had fallen forward at the waist, his head hung down and the damage to the back of his skull was visible to Jim as a dark moist mass of inside stuff exposed to the outside world. He wore long khaki shorts—maybe army issued—and a black T-shirt turning blacker and slicker. His left fist was clenched on his thigh and his right hand seemed to have been violently thrust forward partially under his left thigh. His right index finger was visible and was hooked awkwardly in the trigger of a handgun that lay beneath his legs. The finger was broken backward in the opposite direction of the middle joint.

Jim re-routed his vision to Nina's bare feet. Her toenails had a deep pink polish on them that flattened against her sun-tanned skin. Silence swirled in Jim's ears, his deafness creating so much noise and interference. She had blue jeans on and Jim thought maybe they were Lise's, remembering something Lise had said about them borrowing jeans from each other.

She wore a purple tank top that said Hawaii in a script that Jim thought of as being Hawaiian. There were bright pink flowers below the lettering. Her arms were filled with tattoos, bright and faded, black and colorful. Jim thought of those embroidered samplers Sarah ooh-ed at in antique shops on the Cape—letters and numbers to help us learn.

Hadn't Lise said that Nina was just thinking about getting tat-toos? Or did she have small ones and was thinking about a big one—he couldn't remember the details of the conversation. Was it the day before or the day before that?

Jim shifted his head to include Jen in his sights. She stared back at him, something pulling at the corners of her mouth, as if they didn't know whether to turn up or down. Lise had a small phone to her ear and was mumbling into it. Jim couldn't hear what she was saying, but he could sense there was something official going on. Lise stood straight, her eyes were clear—they offered some lightness and depth now—and her gaze took in every detail of the two bodies on the bed as she spoke into the phone.

This had all started with a phone call, in the middle of the night, in the middle of his life. The phone thrust into his hand in the night, his feet landing on the floor, Cath's voice, and the search for Nina began. He had moved then and kept moving, to New York, then across the country, from Burbank to Sierra Madre to this place in the desert, always moving toward death. Of course Nina was dead. Jim had dicked around, stalled, gotten lost, even as he'd tried so hard to move quickly and in a straight line.

"Nina," whispered Jim, his lips moving around the word. "I'm here." He adjusted the backpack strap on his shoulder.

Nina's arms reached to the places she'd been, the Wicklows, the past. He found Diana and Brooklyn quickly on Nina's left arm. A crescent moon hung over the letters BK and the numbers that Jim thought indicated Diana's birth date. Curlicued Mom entwined with Diana and a green-brown flower—no, it was a tree of some kind. There was a cluster of names and filigree on her left bicep that belonged to Aunt Cath. The IVF twins were named, as was Craig, enclosed in pink geometric shapes and greenish vines. There were small faded clusters of design all along her left arm connected by strings of lines and arrows. These were interrupted by initials and numbers Jim sensed had something to do with the army and Iraq. There were characters he was sure were Arabic or maybe Hebrew. He picked out individual images and names and then adjusted his weird focus, pulling back to see the broad tapestry of the arm, the illustrations blurring into what seemed like an outer sleeve Nina had simply slipped into.

Nina's right arm held Jim's immediate world. J.J. and Emily, their faces, names and birth dates entwined in leaves and flowers and cityscapes. J.J.—Nina's near twin cousin—got special treatment. A small radiating sun made the two J's glow with a yellow outline. The L of his ex-wife's name remained, a small bird only barely transformed the remaining letters, leaving them readable beside a small scripted Sarah. On Nina's right bicep and extending up to the round of her right shoulder, Jim found himself. James R Wicklow in crisp clear letters, upper and lower case, stacked on top of each other and encircled with thorny roses and small white wings. It didn't look like his name even though he recognized it immediately. Where was Ryan?

Jim's vision wobbled, blinking in and out. He still couldn't hear. He found himself on her arm again and realized the tattoo continued under the strap of her tank top and across the top of her breast. This was where he found Ryan amid more thorny vines, flowers and wings spreading from below her shirt up to her chest and shoulder, spiraling down below the shirt toward her breast and her heart below. This was Nina telling the Wicklows who they were.

Jim lifted his eyes to her face. How could she look like this when she was in this state? Her eyes were closed and her face was smooth and still and gave no sign of disruption. She looked both young and old. Her mouth was slightly open, her lips parted, but her jaw didn't appear slack. Her face still had energy although no color, no warmth. There was no visible damage except for a small circle of grey-black at one temple. Her head leaned back over the top of the pillows and it seemed whole although the headboard behind her had deep fractures in it just behind her head. She was still and she was gone, but she didn't seem ruined.

Jim had held her as a baby. He was sure of it. He had held J.J. and Emily and Cath's twins and he had held Nina. He liked holding babies, touching their soft plump arms, making them react in their newborn confusion—they didn't know whether to laugh or cry at what the new world offered them. Underneath the tattoos—if he could only erase them—there was baby Nina, soft and unsure, crying and laughing.

Jim scanned the room for the gun. He very much wanted to find it. His eyes quickly latched onto it on the floor, partially hidden by the bed skirt. He wrenched his feet from the floor and stepped to it. He bent down, reaching.

All at once Lise was crouching over him, grabbing his forearm and pulling his hand back from the gun. "Crime scene," she sputtered.

They remained where they were for more than a moment, Lise embracing him, restraining him. Jim twisted his neck to look at Nina from this odd angle. He saw the damage now. Most of the back of her head was gone, just gone like a sheer drop off a cliff. There was blood all over her neck and back and the tops of her shoulders, which he had mistaken for shadows. He could see the tank top was originally a lighter color now darkened with blood. The pillows held bits of Nina's skull and soft tissue. Jim blinked his eyes and Nina became a corpse. He could see there was no heartbeat, no breath, no pulse, no Nina. He could see the death.

Jim shook off Lise, straightened up and walked around the foot of the bed. There were too many doors and he paused. He stared into the long mirror on what he realized was the bathroom door. He could see himself, Lise and the bodies on the bed all reflected there. The man to your left and the man to your right. He had failed utterly and repeatedly in these simple responsibilities.

He roused himself, adjusted the backpack on his shoulder, found the correct door and left the room. He went the wrong way down the corridor, but got his bearings and reversed back to the living room.

Danny and Jen stood in the kitchen and Jim had the feeling he had interrupted their conversation even though they didn't seem to be talking. They stared at him and he looked away, walking into the kitchen, drawn to the dull light over the stove. He bowed his head, wondered if they thought he was praying and then lowered his eyelids until they were closed. Microscopic flashes burst in the grey of his darkened sight. He felt his lashes on his cheeks and he tried to hear, wondering if the deafness would clear, if his breathing would return.

He felt poisoned, filled once again with the toxins of the terrible world. He'd gotten clean and now wondered what was the point. He made a decision, let effort go and gave into the desire to go down. He was tired of resisting these forces that had been dragging at him for so long. He opened his eyes and reached for one of the still-full whiskey bottles. As his hand closed around its neck he saw Danny and Jen gaze at him in wonder, oblivious witnesses to his fall.

He twisted off the metal cap with a satisfying snap and put the smooth glass opening to his lips. He swallowed the acidy warm liquid. Danny and Jen resumed their weird whispering. Jim took another sip of the whiskey he couldn't believe he was drinking. Nothing happened except that he felt better.

## TWENTY-ONE

Lise went for her phone as they moved down the hall.

The closer Jen's car had pulled them to Palm Desert, the more certain Lise was of what they would find. She had retreated deeper into her secret knowledge with each exit they passed. And as she flipped the light switch on the wall and followed Jim into the bedroom, she had reached into the back right pocket of her jeans—Nina's jeans—and extracted the phone.

She selected the Emergency Call option for the first time ever, telling the phone menu that yes, she was sure she wanted to make an emergency call.

Lise's brain ordered itself, synapses sparked, connections that had seemed to be in permanent failure suddenly found their meeting points. Her experience, her skills, her vocabulary—all the right words, in the right order—they all found proper purpose in the presence of the damaged and the dead.

"My name is Lise Sheridan," she said into the phone. "I want to report two dead bodies, soldiers who have killed themselves with guns."

The 911 operator asked her location.

"I'm in a gated community in Palm Desert. I'm not sure of the name of the complex, but the street address is—" Lise said the numbers.

The 911 operator asked if she was sure.

"Yes, that's the address, and they're dead from self-inflicted GSWs."

The 911 operator asked her how she knew.

"I'm a registered nurse, an ER nurse. They're dead. I can see the wounds. And the guns are here."

The 911 operator asked her if anyone on the premises was armed.

"No, they shot themselves. We found them."

The 911 operator asked about the bodies.

"They're discharged soldiers from the army."

The 911 operator asked which army.

"The U.S. Army. She fought in Iraq. I think he was in Afghanistan."

The 911 operator asked for the names of the people Lise was with.

Lise knew and said everyone's name even as she reached down to tell Jim not to touch the gun.

The 911 operator seemed concerned about what was happening at Lise's location.

"It's just a grieving relative. He's in shock."

The 911 operator wanted to know about the guns again.

"No one is armed here. Are you sending someone?"

"Police and emergency medical services are on the way, ma'am," the 911 operator told her.

"The emergency is over," said Lise.


Lise stayed in the bedroom, watching Jim walk away from Nina. She wanted to sit on the edge of the bed, maybe hold Nina's foot, tell her it would be okay, but she knew better. And there were more phone calls to make.

She stood looking at the bodies, knowing she knew these former people, but there was nothing present that felt like people anymore. Nina was gone, receding into memory. And the man beside her wasn't even the sniper Lise had worried about. Lise knew him from Nik's parties, but couldn't retrieve the sound of his voice. She didn't think she had ever seen Nina and him together, although Lise could remember the soldier's large hand resting on a woman's hip. Was this the scene she had almost pictured—Nina in a bad place. She hadn't wanted to believe it, but here it was, making her believe.

Nina and this other soldier were now simply body parts with the mark of something having left them. Lise remembered this impression from St. Anthony's ER and the Cash. Bodies without whatever it was that made them more than bodies. The closer she had gotten to the dead, the less there was of them. This absence was overwhelming as if it was part of the natural world around her. It felt like getting lost in the woods, surrounded by infinity.

She knew Danny was in the doorway of the room, head bowed to his notebook as he scribbled, trying not to look at the bodies, not knowing what to say. She walked the three steps to him, put herself into his arms and covered his eyes with her hand.

"You don't need to look. Please don't look," Lise told him.

His chest collapsed with small relief and he put his forehead to her neck. She wasn't sure, but she thought he thanked her, moving his lips to form the words but not actually uttering them.


Jen tried to explain to Lise. "I couldn't stay in there."

Lise told her it was fine, there was no reason for Jen to feel she had to endure this.

"I saw enough to tell her mother," added Jen.

Lise was irritated with how everything was stopping and starting, and with these people feeling they needed to make the effort to look at the dead.

"Where's Jim?" Lise needed a new mission.

Jen shifted her head in a weird nod to the glass door, slid open to the outside world.

When Lise stepped out into the night she found it quieter than she expected. She thought she should hear far-off chatter and clinking of glasses, like in a movie when people leave a party that's still going.

Jim sat on one of the outdoor lounge chairs, the webbed back propped up so the whiskey wouldn't dribble down his chin when he drank. Nina's backpack lay in his lap. He looked up at Lise, seemed determined not to speak yet held her gaze until it was time to take another sip.

"You should probably have some water with that," she told him. "It's the desert. You'll get dehydrated."

"I'll keep that in mind," he slurred slightly, trying to correct his uneven speech as soon as he heard it. He narrowed his eyes, squinting with slight embarrassment but resolved in his action. He took a small sip from the bottle.

"We're going to make some phone calls, her mom, the Sierra Madre detective. Maybe Nik."

Jim raised his eyebrows, but seemed uninterested in offering a verbal verdict on any of this.

"Will you want to talk to Nina's mom?"

Jim moved the features of his face in a kind of answer.

"There're going to be a lot of people here in the next few minutes. Cops, EMTs, a coroner. They're going to ask questions. They'll probably be rude in the beginning because they'll be scared by what's happened here, because there are guns. They may want to frisk you. Just take it in stride." Lise knew she was right about all this. "They're going to be here for a long time."

"You're the expert. I'll just follow orders." Jim smiled one of Lise's fake smiles at her.

The swirling red lights bathed them and suddenly there were uniformed men and women moving swiftly through the condo, taking it over, bringing the official world with them.

Lise was the spokesperson. She explained who the dead and the living were. She repeated the information for uniformed people, then people in civilian clothes who were not civilians, then to uniformed medical people, then lawyers. Then she translated for Jen and Danny. She explained Jim to the police and one of the detectives told a uniformed officer to watch over him in the lounge chair. The officer stood in the doorway with one leg in the condo and one on the patio, one hand cupping the butt of his holstered weapon. Everyone seemed to agree that Jim needed watching, but they let him keep the bottle.

Lise felt herself returning from somewhere she had been, maybe for years. Her words pulled her, bringing her back. Her words ordered everything and they seemed to be everywhere, surrounding her, filling her, returning her.

There were so many people working in the condo. It felt like a factory, everyone with a different function, an assembly line production of what happens after. Jen and Danny shrank back to the chairs surrounding the dining table. They were interviewed and abandoned. Lise stood at the end of the hallway and watched people move back and forth, in and out of the bedroom. There was so much equipment, so many tools, in large awkward metal boxes. So many efficient, trained people doing their specialized work—keeping themselves apart in their latex gloves—barely there as people, like the dead they administered to.

When the Sierra Madre detective arrived, Lise realized how long they'd been there.

"I'm sorry it worked out this way, Sheridan," he said in that way that reminded her he had predicted this. "I couldn't reach Nik. Maybe you should try him later." The detective blended in with the other officials, muttering, writing in small notebooks, putting objects in clear plastic envelopes.

Jen held a phone that looked like the new one Danny had. She waved it at Lise, held it in her palm as if it was too hot to hold. Lise took it, put it to her ear and heard the voice she remembered as Nina's mother. Diana was still talking as if Jen was on the line. Lise let her go on for a few phrases before gently interrupting her.

"It's Lise Sheridan. Can I answer any questions for you?"

Diana had no words left so Lise gave them to her. Lise said every phrase about death and dying she had ever learned. She channeled Major Beck and Nik and every wounded soldier who had moved through the Cash. She mouthed VA homilies and commanding officer platitudes. She retrieved fragments of poetry, movie dialogue, something she thought her father had said when her grandfather died. There were new words too, refreshed language that came from Lise newly born into the world. Diana's nonsense sobbing stilled and settled into a thick silence and then coherent gratitude. She asked Lise if she could put Jim on the phone because his sister wanted to speak to him.

Lise and the officer exchanged understanding nods as she moved across the threshold of the sliding doors to the patio. The officer stood by while Lise offered the phone to Jim.

"For me?" Jim asked, his eyes searching through the short distance to Lise's.

"Your sister," Lise said, lifting the flat phone toward him.

"Pick up the phone, Jimmy," Cath crackled, through a thousand filters of grief and distance and the phone's muted speaker function. Jim and Lise both stared at the device. Cath's voice was so far away. Jim took the phone from Lise, but it slipped from his hand into his lap. He stared down at it, fumbled for it before getting a firm grasp, and then put it to his ear. He straightened his back and opened his mouth as if he was going to speak but he said nothing. He looked up at Lise. Then he placed the phone back into her open palm, relaxing his spine, sitting back in defeat, clutching the backpack. He shook his head, he didn't want this conversation.

Lise pushed the speaker icon and Cath could be heard more clearly now. "Jimmy, pick up, pick up the fucking phone. Will you talk to me? Sarah's here." Lise gave Jim her cold hard stare and in response he settled back deeper into the chair and his drinking.

"I can't talk to the women. Go away," Jim spewed, curling himself around the bottle and the backpack.

"Jimmy, please. Jesus, you fuck, are you drinking?"

Lise released the speaker and put the phone to her ear, walking off into the deep dark of the lawn beyond the patio.

"It's Lise Sheridan. I'm sorry, but he's kind of out of it."

There was silence and then: "I'm sorry, but who are you?"

Lise stopped walking, letting her eyes get used to the new darkness away from the homes. Slowly things came into focus, shapes formed as her eyes found a way to see. She was on a golf course. The grass under her borrowed sneakers was groomed short and dense. She saw a pole with a flag sticking in the ground ahead of her. She sat down on the damp ground. Night dew in the desert.

"I was a friend of Nina's."

"I'm sorry. I'm Nina's Aunt Cath. Is it horrible? It's horrible, isn't it? Diana's taking more pills—not too many. Jimmy's drunk, right? His wife didn't think he would."

Lise and Cath talked in that matter-of-fact tone of two people who had seen people behave in all the ways that human beings can behave. Neither revealed anything but the facts of their lives and recent events. It was understood that Lise did not have to look out for Jim, that whatever destruction he had in mind, Lise had silent permission from Cath to let him fall.

"I don't miss Ryan as much as I should," Cath admitted. "Not as much as I say."

"Because he's kind of always there," Lise guessed.

"Yes," was all Cath said. There was silence for some long moments. "I was going to say it must be late, but then I remembered it's earlier there."

Lise looked around. There was a lit window in only a few homes. Jen's condo was too bright with too much activity for the hour. "It's late everywhere," Lise said.

"My niece wants to talk to you for a minute," Cath said all in a rush.

Lise was confused. Wasn't Nina her niece?

"Jim's daughter Emily. She'd like a word," Cath said to clarify. "Is that all right?"

Lise said that it was and then she heard a high voice roughed up by too much information.

"Hi, I'm Emily Wicklow."

Lise introduced herself for the eleventh or twelfth time in the last few hours.

"Were you in Iraq with Nina?"

"I was there, but not with her."

"Were you friends?"

Lise said they were.

"Are you very sad?"

Lise said she was.

"I'm very sad too. Everyone here is very sad."

Lise said it was all very sad, that Emily's dad was very sad too.

"Sometimes my dad lives like he wants to die."

Lise snapped alert, her robot brain focused, her ears strained to hear Emily's voice.

"You know what I mean? Not that he does anything about it. He just walks around with this want, you know?"

Lise knew exactly. "It's okay. He's okay."

"How are you, Lise?"

"I'm good, Emily, thanks for asking. How about you?"

"Everyone here is taking pills to deal, but I think I'm just going to take a really hot shower and then go to sleep. Do you think that's okay?"

"I think that's more than okay," Lise said, breathing automatically in and out, lifting her eyes to the night sky for the first time. There were stars in the blackness, just a few, but they were visible.

"Could we stay in touch?" Emily asked.

Lise said her email address and Emily said she would write her when she had something to say. They said goodbye and ended the call.

Lise could see the technicians, police and other officials packing up, leaving the condo. And then slowly she realized that she was watching body bags moving across her line of sight. Men in dark jumpsuits, four of them, badges clipped to their chests, held an end of each of the two long black bags. They moved them from the hallway through the living room and out the front door where Lise lost sight of them. The black shapes floated through the light, moving along a horizon line as if they were bobbing along the surface of an ocean. The bags had seemed momentarily filled with the fading energies of lost life and gone people, but then they turned inanimate again, returning to the flat, inert nothings that guys in uniforms could thrust into the back of a van.

She saw Danny and Jen turn away from the black bags. She saw them standing in the light of the open doors, staring out into the dark either at Jim or beyond looking for her. She would head back inside soon, but she wanted another few minutes to herself if only to marvel at her slow repair.

She used her phone to dial Nik's number. She would wait until morning to call Major Beck. The call to Nik rang and rang and did not go to voicemail. Lise listened to the ringing and watched the sky become a shade lighter. The night was gone.

## TWENTY-TWO

Danny pushed Record on the camera in his head. He would just watch and absorb now. He knew what he was observing, knew how to store it for later. He had run out of notebook paper anyway. He sat at the dining table with Jen, looking from her to the wider scene and back again.

"Have you ever seen anything like that?" he asked her.

"There wasn't that much blood or open, you know, wounds," answered Jen.

"Still."

"I've given birth." Jen tightened her lips. "There's more blood and goop than you can imagine. It's everywhere, a real mess."

Danny never really thought about the women he knew having babies, actually giving birth. He couldn't connect the visual dots to anyone he knew. It wasn't the blood he was talking about anyway. "You've never seen a corpse or a cadaver or whatever before, neither of us, so don't, you know..." He trailed off again, wondering if they were one-upping each other on the shit they'd seen.

Danny watched the uniformed people do their competent thing. He watched Lise, seemingly stronger, clearer, talking the official language with these strangers. He was scared. The chilly waves of uncertainty—this was fear. He was like that guy at the end of that movie, approaching the innermost worst or whatever that screenwriting book had called it. He was the guy who was afraid.

He lacked credentials for this crime scene. He tried to catalogue the violence he'd seen, where he'd used it in scripts. He'd seen little violence in his life and certainly no dead bodies. There was the occasional attempt at fighting in college. He was always a spectator, watching his dorm mates go at each other. There was always some physical guy, who pulled the fighters apart, shaking his head in disappointment.

He'd seen a bar fight in the Bronx once between two men he didn't know—he'd gone for beers after a Yankee game. There had been cracked bones and blood and what he recognized to be precision moves by trained boxers.

He'd seen his own blood too. Just last year he'd received an errant basketball pass to the face in a Beverlywood pick-up game and there had been pain and extremely red blood. A soap opera actor had applied an ice pack to his bruised but unbroken face.

In the subway cars back in New York, there would sometimes be homeless people sleeping still for so long that Danny feared they might be dead. And then they would inevitably move a limb or somehow indicate they were alive. He would look away with relief. No, he had never seen a dead body before.

He noticed the precise movements, the fragments of lingo from the people working in the condo. They formed little sparks of recognition in him, telling details he could hang his writer's hat on. He made up backstory for everyone in the room, but when he came to Lise he stopped. Was she the story?

Danny blanked his mind, closed the file on the in-progress feature film and opened a fresh document in the Final Draft software in his head. He needed to make Lise's world manageable, dole it out in self-contained highly-structured doses. The answer came to him the way nothing had ever come to him, with small tingles down his spine that signaled the opposite of fear. This world was made for television.

He wondered if Lise would consent to a reality show. He wouldn't have to write as much that way.

"This is some reality show," Danny tried with Jen.

"Are you kidding? Who would watch this?" Jen looked at Danny like he was the softest man she had ever met. "What happened to you?" she asked.

"I was joking, being ironic." He was glad he had checked. This had to be fictional, shaped, ordered. The camera could shake—a touch of hand-held would add authenticity—but it had to look good. This was how it could be packaged.

"Marco's taking us back to New York," Jen said out of nowhere. "We've decided to go back."

"That's big news. You going back to an agency?" Danny didn't feel the tug he expected. Maybe he had gotten away for good.

"Looks like we need the money and this place isn't going to sell now," said Jen, a break of pained humor spreading across her face. "I fucked up," she added, as a revision.

Danny felt the harshness between them dissolve. He dropped his shoulders and turned up the palm of his right hand. "Probably not as much as you think." Danny didn't want to have this conversation right now. He was busy making up dialogue, figuring out scenes.

"I need to start over," Jen insisted.

"So you'll do that," Danny said. He thought of all the ad agency people they knew who had fallen beneath the wheels, turned into irredeemable assholes or disappeared for twenty-eight days only to return busted down to boring. Maybe there was a character in there for the new show.

Jen turned from him and spoke to one of the passing technicians. "Are you done with the kitchen? I need to clean something."

There was a conference among two men in suits and the technician and then Jen got her permission. She left Danny alone at the dining table. He was okay on his own, he had plenty to think about. He hit Pause and closed his eyes, powered down his ears, and rested. Just for a few minutes. But then he felt more afraid or bold or something that made him want to find Lise.

Danny gingerly stepped past the uniformed officer, not really meeting his eyes, staring at the guy's hand on the butt of his holstered weapon, keeping his own hands in full view.

Danny thought Jim looked like a comic strip version of a Depression-era bum drinking from a jug marked XXX. When he saw Danny he straightened his posture, swung his shoes to the patio slate and put the bottle down. Danny watched him figure out what to do with his hands before he shoved them into his jacket pockets.

"Where's Lise?" Danny asked. It was the only thing he wanted to know.

Jim didn't answer.

"Dude." Danny didn't want to say his name or become friends. "Where is she?"

"On the phone," Jim said, very slowly. "That way," he added, even slower, shifting to face the dark of the golf course.

Danny stared out into the night, hoping his eyes would adjust, discover their super powers and find her out there in the dark.

"I'm having trouble seeing," Jim said, talking at normal speed now. "And hearing."

"I don't need to know this," Danny said, although he thought it was good material. Maybe he should listen a little more to New York Man, if he could keep his distance, not let him get to him. He thought though that he should offer condolences or say something formal about Nina. He hadn't really learned how these things were said, he realized, except for writing them for other people to say. When did you learn these things?

"I'm sorry about Nina," he said. "I knew her, met her a few times."

"Yeah, thanks." Jim responded in a way that sounded automated. "She was nice."

"It's a shock. It'll be a shock for her mom." Danny thought he heard Jim mutter something like "again", but he wasn't sure.

"This is the sad part," Danny added, although he meant to say that Nina was sad. It had just come out wrong.

Jen transformed the living room with cleaning products and their smells, but Danny still felt the death from that bedroom wafting. Jen microwaved enchiladas from the freezer. They ate a kind of stand-up meal at the kitchen counter. He couldn't bring himself to drink from any of the bottles, knowing Nina and the other dead body had touched them. He sipped beer from a small glass Mia had probably used for morning apple juice. He tried to breath and sip and talk and move as if people hadn't killed themselves just down the hall.

Danny closed his eyes as he forked pieces of enchiladas into his mouth. He didn't want to see the red salsa or the melted cheesy swirl. The four of them huddled around the kitchen counter on their feet, eating what they could get down, drinking more. Jim stood unstable on his legs, wobbling but staying upright. Jen tended to him in a cool manner, probably the way she helped Mia do things.

Lise scraped her plate clean, drew her teeth across her fork, and then left the counter. Danny watched her walk slowly down the hall and pause at the first bedroom. She didn't look in to see where the bodies had been, she just dropped her chin slightly and stood very still. Then she moved on down the hall. She turned left and disappeared from view.

Danny followed her, leaving Jen and Jim to each other. He held his breath even as he wondered if there was anything to smell in that first bedroom. He wondered if Lise was asleep or if she wanted sex. He left his little glass of beer on a side table and went down the hall.

He found Lise curled on the bed, fully-clothed, deeply asleep as if she'd had a very long day. Danny crawled gently onto the bed, toeing off his sneakers, letting them fall quietly to the carpeted floor. He lay beside her, resting, wondering if she would need him.

# TWENTY-THREE

Jim woke on the sectional couch thirstier than he had ever been in his life. His brain, muscles, skin felt dehydrated, sucked of all moisture. And then there was the pain in his head. And his metallic tongue.

Small thoughts of deliberate breathing and purposeful movement came to him slowly, entering his mind at the center and then blossoming outward into complete comprehension. He followed these orders and felt his chest moving up and down, his arms moving toward his torso.

His left arm wouldn't obey. He slowly turned his head to see why. Jen lay on top of his arm, her body on its back on the other part of the couch, at a ninety-degree angle to him. All her buttons were buttoned and her zippers were zipped. At least he hadn't done that.

He tugged his arm out from under her and sat up in one motion. He was immediately flooded by a tsunami of nausea. Acidy vapors filled his throat. He planted his feet on the floor, his elbows on his thighs, his head in his hands, and begged the hurt to ease. His left arm throbbed with ache.

The curtains hanging in front of the sliding doors protected him from the brassy morning sun, but between the hanging fabric he could see the desert rays thrusting themselves like spotlights into the room. He turned away from the dusty dark TV screen. He didn't want it on. He had all the information he needed.

He moved slowly into the kitchen space. He was grateful that it was so clean and grasped at a fleeting vision of Jen washing dishes. He turned on the cold water and stuck his mouth under the faucet. The instant the liquid hit his insides it came back up, dragging with it the searing contents of his stomach. He heaved and convulsed, vomiting into the sink, watching as the water failed to drive the puke down the drain. He couldn't control the spasms and so he gave himself over to the violent rhythms.

Slowly his body released him from its torque, but the surging nausea remained. He rested his arms on the edge of the sink. He struggled to find his breath and wondered how long he could stay conscious. He jerked his head slightly, like shaking off a mosquito. His vision skidded one way and then the other and then settled. He felt faint.

Nina. The name came to him all at once, reminding him of his whole life and the last three days, and how he had come to stand in a desert condo, the world betraying him. Had he failed in his mission? He'd found her, but too slowly. Could he have stopped her, could he have gotten to her in time, gotten her home? Ryan would have.

Diana had said they were so alike. Ryan and Nina. Raising their left hands in the air when they gave directions, dreamy eyes, hitches in their walks. They hated peas. They were both gone from him. Diana would slap him—no, that wasn't her. She had predicted this and wouldn't blame him. It would be Cath who would hit him, beat him with her little fists, open her palm and smack his face. She would do it in front of Sarah, who would look on with a look he wouldn't be able to read, then comfort him. The women would take another piece of him and give him back something else.

He missed Sarah and the Cape and the plips on the pond. He urgently wanted to get back there, back to the Rhode Island Reds—minus four. He shook off the images of the killing day. Sarah had weathered it in the end. He had been the one who had wobbled, the blood draining from his head as he watched the chicken guy cut their throats. Jim swore he could smell the blood, feel its syrup in his nostrils. He looked down the hallway to the bedroom. Was it here, in this place too?

He drank more water, letting it trickle from the tap into his hand and sipping it from his palm. He vomited again, this time accepting it. After Ryan, he had wanted to poison himself. When he moved to the Cape, he had wanted to purify himself. Now, in this desert place, he simply wanted relief from existence. Lost people became dead people, he thought.

His swimming dream came back to him. Had he dreamt in the night? Swimming in a basement pool, low ceiling, low light. A flashlight beam swinging across his lane, waking him every night at the same time, though not since he had left the Cape. The warnings had ceased.

His left arm throbbed. He opened and closed the fist at the end of it. This made him feel better. All those kids at Nik's without limbs—or was it just the one? Maxwell or Acevedo? Menacing children, armed with attitude and so many questions. Ryan would have known the right answers, would have done it all smarter, nicer, faster. He would have lived better.

Jim's heart pounded heavily in his chest. Each beat felt like a heavy metal wrench trying to break out of his rib cage. He felt his blood moving through his veins and arteries, his heart pumping the blood through all his spaces. He breathed deeply in and out and felt his lungs working hard to push blood into his heart and out to his greedy cells. Every part of him was in pain.

Jim wanted cool air and hoped he would find it outside. He lumbered through the open sliding door to the patio, passing Jen still asleep on the couch. He felt the cool slate under his feet. He looked down, registered he was barefoot, wondered where his shoes were. He moved quickly to the golf grass beyond, walking away from the condo. The desert morning air was already giving way to a hotter day. He began to sweat, wanted to remove his jacket. His arms twisted in an empty gesture and he realized he was only wearing a shirt.

The blood and the brains of the bedroom came to him and he moved farther from the condo, making his way along the too-lush green. The blades of grass pricked at the soles of his feet. He wanted to walk on the beach, feel his feet slip in the sand. He felt bloated, wondered where his hard body had gone. What were his positions? Could he wait until he relieved himself of his hangover or did he have to know now? How much money did he have? Is today Wednesday?

He had the sense he was watching a movie about the science of his insides and the soundtrack was telling him something dramatic was about to happen. He dreaded it. Doom. His deafness returned, the world echoed hollowly and then went silent. His vision went beige and then blank. Each system in his body flared with force and then powered down.

He fell, folding over on himself, hitting the ground with his knees and then his hips and chest, landing on his side, one arm crushed beneath his weight. The invisible hand reached up through him and grabbed at his throat. The towers fell again, this time with crushing weight on his chest. They fell and fell and the pressure and pain pushed through his skin, through bones and then through his heart. He was going down, going down steps in the dark. And then he disappeared from himself.

## TWENTY-FOUR

"Captain Lise."

"Lise."

"Sheridan."

"Nurse."

The shouts repeated, but in sleep Lise heard only meaningless noise. She wanted to stay away, gone from the bloody mess of the world.

"Sheridan nine-one-one Sheridan." This was Danny she recognized now, saying words she had only seen him type. "Man down Sheridan move it Sheridan."

Now she was awake, swimming up from below.

"He's dying," shouted Jen.

Lise's hands moved in the air as she rolled off the bed. She landed on her feet, grabbing for the nearest object, but came up with empty palms. She opened her eyes. She ran out into the morning light, the brightening desert sky offering nothing to orient her. She saw Jim crumpled on the green and went to him.

She dropped her knees into the grass and went to work.

ABC. Airway Breathing Circulation.

Jim was unconscious. Lise shoved a knuckle in his side and shouted at him. No response. She looked back toward the condo and saw Jen coming toward her already on the phone, saying, "We need an ambulance."

Lise rolled Jim toward her, arranging him so he was flat on his back. He wasn't breathing.

She quickly undid his belt and opened the top button of his pants. Airway.

She gently lifted his chin with one hand, using her other to press on his forehead so his head was tilted back at the correct angle. She swiped her index finger in his mouth, searching for something that might be blocking his breath.

She looked closely at his chest, willing it to rise and fall with breathing. She counted to herself, hoping. One and two and three and four—he still wasn't breathing. She put two fingers to the side of his neck. No pulse. Fuck here we go.

Jen pushed the speaker icon on the phone and put it on the grass near Lise.

"It's the operator from last night. She knows you know what you're doing."

Six seven. "Airway's open. He's not breathing," Lise said toward the phone. "I'm going to give him two breaths."

Breathing.

Lise pinched Jim's nose with her thumb and forefinger. She placed the heel of that same hand on his forehand to keep the head tilted. Her other hand continued to lift his chin.

She inhaled, trying not to do it too deeply.

She locked her lips on his, closed the space with their flesh, creating an airtight seal.

She forced two breathes into him, each one second long.

She did not feel his chest rise on either breath.

She broke the seal between them.

She pulled his shirt up to expose his chest. She adjusted her position in relation to his body, readying herself for what came next.

She double-checked that she was kneeling in a way that would give her the right leverage. She was thirsty and wondered briefly if it was from the night-before booze or the adrenaline now.

Circulation.

"I'm beginning compressions," Lise said to the phone.

With the middle and forefingers of her left hand she located the familiar notch where the lower rims of the rib cage meet in the middle of the chest.

She put the heel of her hand on the breastbone next to the notch. She glanced at his nipples to make sure her hand was between them.

She placed her right hand on top of the left and interlocked the fingers.

She brought her shoulders over his sternum, pressed downward with straight arms. She pushed hard, she pushed fast, stopping and pulling back as she hit what felt like the half-way mark in the depth of his chest. She kept her hands in position, but relaxed pressure after each push.

She pushed, she released, knowing she had to get to thirty before she could push two more breaths into him.

She found the rhythm quickly, but she knew she would tire quickly. Twelve and thirteen fourteen fifteen sixteen seventeen.

"Danny went for aspirin," Jen said.

Twenty twenty-one twenty-two twenty-three.

"Twenty-four twenty-five twenty-six," the 911 operator counted helpfully, her voice coming from the phone in the grass.

Twenty-seven twenty-eight twenty-nine thirty.

Lise stopped the compressions and locked lips again with Jim. She gave him two breaths.

She started the compressions again. One and two and three and four and five and six and.

"Paramedics are thirty seconds out," the operator said. "You should hear sirens."

And ten eleven and twelve thirteen fourteen.

Lise could hear the sirens.

Jen made a noise like she had been trying not to cry and had won.

*Not looking good Captain.*

Eighteen nineteen twenty.

*Hold CPR check for pulse.*

Twenty-one twenty-two twenty-three.

*Step back Captain.*

Twenty-four twenty-five.

*I think we should call it.*

Twenty-six twenty-seven.

*Any suggestions?*

Twenty-eight twenty-nine thirty.

*No sir.*

One and two and.

*Okay let's call this.*

One and two and three and.

*Good try Captain.*

Four and five and six and seven.

*Record the date and time.*

And eight and nine and.

*Specialist Nina Wicklow September 16, 2008.*

Ten eleven twelve.

The paramedic truck erupted out of the golf course toward them. The sirens obliterated everything and underneath her hands Lise felt a change.

Jim's lids lifted and his face opened briefly before fixing into a daze. His arms fumbled in the air and then fell back to the grass.

Lise pulled her hands from him. His chest rose and fell. His heart beat.

"Fuck," Jen said. "Did you just do that?"

The siren cut off in mid-wail and Lise heard the truck doors open, the rattle of the gurney wheels.

The paramedics moved Lise away, inserting themselves.

Lise pushed herself to standing and Jen put her arms around her so she wouldn't fall. Danny pressed a small bottle of orange baby aspirin into Lise's hand.

They watched the paramedics attack Jim with their equipment.

"You okay?" Danny asked Lise.

The question hung amid the muttering of the paramedics, the

sounds of the desert morning around her. Words and numbers came to her and she felt the burden of the things she knew and had lost.

She dropped to the grass, falling through Jen and Danny's arms. She spread her limbs, her hands and feet feeling for space.

Danny and Jen stood above her, creating shadows, blocking the sun. Jen was smile-crying in a gentle way she probably couldn't feel.

"You okay?" Danny asked again, less urgent this time, just making contact.

The bright sun now forced Lise's eyes shut. She held the small aspirin bottle in her hand. She saw the California sky spreading its blue across the world. Palm trees swayed from desert to desert, from the West to the East, stoic above the golf course, shuddering above the Cash. Red Zone smoke rose in the distance. Nina made a gesture in the air with her hand, pointing, giving directions—where?

# AFTER MONEY

## TWENTY-FIVE

Jen spent most of the morning at the hospital with Danny and Lise, sitting in plastic chairs. She returned to the condo, letting herself in with the key Nina had left on the kitchen counter. She sat in the living room and contemplated cleaning the entire place, every room, every inch of it. In the end she called a cleaning service and left the door open for them. She drove back to Sierra Madre alone.

She drove with a blank brain. She wanted to think, but she couldn't form thoughts. The desert filled her, wiping out everything else. She made a lot of stops, bought things she didn't need, didn't want to eat. She used all the twenties. When she got home the smell of smoke from the fire was gone.

Marco and Mia put her to bed in Mia's room. She slept for the rest of the day and part of the evening, content in oblivion. She woke to find Mia sitting by the bed, wearing her quiver of arrows, quick to inhale at her mother's every move. Marco was stretched out on the floor, his long body hanging over the edges of the area rug. Mia had positioned all her plastic animals and people around him. He dozed with his arms crossed on his chest, a willing Gulliver in his daughter's empire.

The next morning Jen sat at the computer with the bag of candy bars and junk food she had acquired on the trip back from Palm Desert. Some of it she had bought, some she had stolen.

She looked around the living room and wondered what they should sell first.

"What do you think?" she asked Marco when he brought her coffee.

"One of the couches can definitely go."

Jen wrote the sales copy, Marco took measurements and pictures, and Mia clicked the Post button on Craigslist. They waited for buyers to send emails, then bring them cash in exchange for their belongings. It felt like the house was leaking, important substances flowing away from them.

Buyers pulled in and out of the driveway. Jen and Marco made long to-do lists and checked off items as they were completed. They listed the houses, reduced the price on the condo, sold one car immediately and arranged to sell the other when they left. Mia was willing to part with a surprising portion of her stuff, explaining very seriously that she was ready for a life whack.

"It's hack, Bean, not whack," Marco gently corrected her.

"I want a whack," Mia insisted.

"If she wants a life whack, let her have a life whack," was all Jen could manage to say.

Jen found it difficult to part with specific belongings, conducting a psychic tango in her head until she could post the item for sale. Several pairs of designer shoes, the four Eames chairs and the Trek bicycle she never rode, fell into this category. She watched their neighbor's teenager pedal the bike away and felt something like anger. How did they get here? Slowly and all at once was all she could think.

"I loved those chairs," she admitted to Marco. They stood around the table, wondering where they would sit when they ate.

"The weather's okay. We can sit outside for dinner." Marco said.

"It's too hot," she said, wanting to resist all solutions.

"Cool nights in the desert, babe. Remember?"

What couldn't be sold but was still unseemly to own, they gave to St. Rita's. Jen split their utensils in half and found they still had twelve forks, knives and spoons. They had too many plates and bowls, place mats and table cloths, sheets and towels, too many wine glasses. When they carried the boxes into the basement hall of the church, Jen felt the transforming tingle of déjà vu. She had been there before, bearing the news of where Nina could be found. The idea returned of being responsible for the missing and the dead.

She thought she should apologize to Marco when the bearded man from Arcadia came for the Triumph. She was to blame, she had pulled them all into this mindlessness. But when she said the words, Marco looked at her as if she still wasn't listening to him, as if she hadn't seen anything at all.

The man from Arcadia paid with a wedge of crisp hundreds for the Triumph and rode it away, his short brother following in a green SUV. Marco wouldn't talk, didn't want to play with Mia or Mommy. He went for a run to get over it and returned to the house smelling like he'd smoked a joint.

After-images from the desert invaded Jen's sleep. Jim hovered over Nina, her head a bloody stump. Jen felt gravity pulling her down, the pale green carpeting of the desert condo rising around her ankles, gripping at her. The visual plane of the dreamscape shifted to an unsustainable angle and she woke, jerked back into the conscious world. She got out of bed to check on Mia and re-check the doors and windows of the strange house. She stood in the hall, staring at the front door, wondering if she should open it.

She returned to bed, waking Marco, finding her desire for him again—finally. She whispered money talk to him while they made love.

"We're solving money problems with money," she said into his chest.

"That's how you solve them," he said to her neck.

"But we're poor."

"We are very not poor. We just have debt."

"Everything sold so fast."

"It all had value. We couldn't afford it. Someone else can."

"It feels like we're cheating. Shouldn't it be harder to fix this?"

The question worried her as she put her lips to his stomach.

## TWENTY-SIX

Lise stood at Jim's bedside and gripped his hand in hers as he struggled to remain conscious in the sedating atmosphere of the C.C.U.. She translated doctor-speak to Jim, and to Sarah and Emily when they arrived. He'd had a cardiac event in that his heart stopped and then was started again. They'd found and removed three blockages with the new less-invasive surgery, and he would be good to go soon—these things were easy to translate. She was efficient, knowledgeable and walked quickly away when she needed to be alone. Everyone in the cardiac care unit had all their limbs.

Danny left her in Palm Desert shortly after Jen drove home. His eagerness to get away from the hospital, to get to where he could write whatever it was he had to write—this impressed her.

"I'm sorry. I have to go."

"Stop apologizing. Just go."

"I'm not breaking up with you. I just have to get back to my place."

Lise wondered what he thought he might be ending by leaving.

"I'll wait for his family," she said, waving him away.

Emily, when she arrived, seemed astonishingly young to Lise. She was practical and unpretentious, but seemed open to the world in a way that Lise feared required a kind of protection the child was not getting.

"Don't be afraid of how pasty he is," she said to Emily, but Emily assured her she was fully Googled with info and knew what to expect.

"I like that you're good at what you did, know how to do that kind of important stuff," said Emily, launching into one of her many gratitude-athons that made Lise stare at the waxy floor.

"It's just what people do," Lise said, many times.

"It's not what anyone I know knows how to do."

They left Sarah and Jim alone, watching them at a distance, seeing Sarah try to figure out how to care for him, talk to him, let him be. Lise liked Sarah, the way she moved like a distance runner, quick and long-legged, eating up floor by gliding along on her worn-in sneakers.

"She's exactly like my mom," Emily said. "Just less pissed off."

Lise liked hearing about Jim from Emily. It made him sound less like the man she watched stand over Nina, realizing how late he was—as if it would have made a difference. Soon Lise felt extra and unneeded so she extracted herself from Emily's constant reaching. Nik answered his phone on the first ring.

"I had the landline ported to the cell," he explained. "Seeing as how the fire ate the landline—"

Lise had never heard Nik complain about his own shit before.

"I need to go home," she said.

"I'll send someone," Nik said, hanging up, getting back to his problems.

Maxwell and Acevedo drove her Jetta down to the hospital, bringing Jim's bag in the trunk. Lise left the Wicklows and drove up to Joshua Tree with the guys, delaying her return to the world.

Maxwell lit the bowl with his Zippo. The flame pulsed in the still air.

"Inhale brother," Maxwell said. "You're next," he added to Lise.

Acevedo held the pipe to his lips with his only hand, inhaling slowly and deeply, his eyes wide.

"Your turn Captain," Maxwell said, but Lise shook him off. She swallowed the last of her fourth or fifth beer and leaned her head back against the plastic webbing of the chair.

The motel building threw a shadow over them. They had pulled their chairs into the shade, away from the fading blue of the swimming pool. The tourist couples and traveling families knew to stay away from them. Lise could feel them keeping their lives apart from her and the guys, making sure not to offend or disturb. Lise wondered how dangerous she really looked. A guy from motel management came by twice to ask them to only drink, not smoke. He acted like he'd been through this before.

Lise watched the motel guy walk around the edges of the pool, retreating to his boss's office and the list of rules he didn't like enforcing. To Lise he was just another alien, like the happy people in the swimming pool, like Maxwell and his videogame rat-a-tat and Acevedo and his empty limb—all strangers, making her feel foreign.

"It's hot," Maxwell said.

"It's the desert yo," Acevedo answered.

"Why are we always in the desert?" Lise asked, meaning it every way she could think of. "I need to get out of here."

"Home?" Maxwell asked, but Lise didn't know how to answer.

They talked about everyone they knew who had died. No one mentioned Nina.

They remembered him and her and then him again and that haji and this translator and that medic and the gunner and that dude who was definitely CIA or doing something he shouldn't and then blam down he went and there was blood and sand and everyone yelling and then quiet too quiet like in the movies only nothing bad happened and then incoming and they saw the smoke in the red zone and it was go time and they were rushing-rushing bringing them into the Cash and the slow-motion slowness of stabilizing and surgery and it's going to be okay you're going to be okay.

The three of them drank and smoked to a near hallucinatory state. Lise gave in when she ran out of beer, sucking down the peppery smoke, letting it fill her head and making the missed connections seem purposeful. They ordered pizza and answered the door in their underwear and ate it sitting on the large bed

Acevedo's missing arm set her off, triggering her own loss and fear, the tears coming in vicious spurts that made her whole body spasm. The cycle started again: feeling sure and in control, and then losing it, flinching at everything, wanting to obliterate herself. Language left her completely. She lay between them, her lips on Acevedo's stump while he sobbed openly. Maxwell embraced her from behind, one hand on a breast, the other in her hair. She didn't believe the words they said to her and she didn't feel what they said they were feeling. She wanted to feel, if that was the word. She wanted to feel after she saved the man's life, but there was nothing, just blue sky and palm trees. She wanted to feel and when she didn't she wanted to be away from them.

Lise slept all day and woke sober, clear and hungry.

At night she drove them back to Sierra Madre. The radio blasted head-banging metal so Lise didn't have to listen to them debate nonsense in the back seat.

They stopped for burritos at some exit in the dark in between towns. There were voicemails from Emily on Lise's phone. Jim was still alive, his heart beating. Lise pushed the buttons that erased the messages.

# TWENTY-SEVEN

Jim woke up in the C.C.U., feeling the grip of Lise's hand. She came and went in a haze of doctors, nurses and machines and post-surgical alienation. She was then replaced by Emily and Sarah. All the women held his hand, urging him to stay, wake, recognize them, please live.

He watched TV endlessly in his room and in the hallways as he rolled his IV during his corridor laps. He could read the systems again now, understand the information on the screens. Sometimes he would pause in his linoleum walks, lose time and find himself overwhelmed with grief and failure unable to stop the intrusive images of Nina, broken and dead. He felt like he was watching the world come to an end—again—as if people were breaking apart, all the time, everywhere. He had wanted to die again in those moments and take the whole world and all its systems with him. The cardiologist said depression was normal after what his body had been through. It takes time, Mr. Wicklow.

Emily was the one who told him in adoring tones that Lise had performed CPR, bringing him back, saving Jim's life in the most literal sense there was. Jim wasn't sure what to do with this information. He wasn't entirely grateful and couldn't imagine a scenario where he would thank her. At one of the very moments he was figuring out what the protocol might be, Emily said, "I already thanked her a bazillion times so you don't have to. We're going to be friends. You don't have to thank her."

"I'll thank her. I'll send her an email or something," Jim had bluffed.

"Dad, don't be a liar. Be happier." Emily said "liar" like it was just another word.

Jim had hallway laps to do so the conversation ended.

"Can you do the full fifteen minutes today?" Emily asked. She sounded like a nagging nurse already. He feared she would soon tell him that she wanted to be like Lise, learn how to save lives.

As he rolled his IV along the hallway he sorted through experiences that were worth having and those he could just as soon skip. He knew as he made the lists that they were the whiny litanies of a sore loser, but it felt good to be assigning value again. The approving looks of the medical personnel he passed on his shuffling walks filled him with enough loathing to power him through the full fifteen minutes that had been prescribed.

The hospital staff had literally dragged him from his bed within hours of his triple bypass surgery. He was to get on his feet, get dressed, walk for fifteen minutes, learn how to care for his incisions—every day. That this protocol was not considered abuse alarmed him. He wanted to report them to someone in charge, but they were in charge. He did as he was told despite the initial pain and all-consuming terror.

He hated the suntanned, overly-interested tones of the local cardiologist and couldn't wait to get back to what he hoped would be the New York indifference of the Park Avenue heart guy he had been referred to.

"I'm not crazy about your insistence on flying home so soon, but if you'll stay nearby for a week and do a little cardiac rehab, then I won't worry so much." The cardiologist insisted on meeting Jim's eyes when he spoke to him.

"We're good. I'm good. Do you need me to sign something?" Jim asked.

"A nurse will be on that plane with you. We'll be worried about your oxygen levels and dehydration."

Jim had nothing to say. He was getting his way even though it scared the hell out of him.

"Next couple of weeks, just don't lift anything heavy, don't put your arms above your head for too long, get some sleep for Christ sake's. And stay hydrated," the desert doctor said. He rattled off more instructions like he was a card dealer offering commentary on the up cards he was distributing in seven-card stud.

"Sure, thanks," Jim said, although he wasn't sure now, looking at Sarah, wondering why she wasn't insisting he stay in the hospital, that he needed more care. Jim wanted them all to resist his will, maybe even tell him no he couldn't. What kind of hack doctor was this guy? And whose side was Sarah on? Shouldn't Jim's activity be more restricted, shouldn't medical people be taking care of him twenty-four-seven? They had stuck things into his chest, touched his heart for fuck's sake. They didn't do the full filet from stem to stern anymore for his kind of surgery, but it was still heart surgery. And now they were just letting him walk the streets, stay in a hotel, get on an airplane. If this was all that was required after a heart attack and a bypass operation, then maybe he hadn't failed so badly when he went to Sierra Madre. Maybe people didn't expect much of each other anymore.

The nights in the hospital were grinding hard and he would be glad to be rid of them. Machines made more noises than people, young men turned old and old men were wheeled away. On the last night before he was discharged, Sarah made an arrangement with the night nurse and curled up in bed with Jim for a few hours of television.

"We're voting for Obama, aren't we?" Sarah asked after an interview with McCain. "We want smart people solving this mess, don't we babe?"

"Everyone knows McCain and the Bushies are financial knuckleheads. Obama'll have smart guys on it, guys from the Street," Jim explained.

"What about us? You good?" Sarah didn't look at him when she asked this.

Jim thought for an instant he should be careful what he said to her, but then decided not to worry about anything at all.

"No one knows what comes next, not even the smart guys." Jim took a deep breath, mostly to check if he still could. "If it all blows up and you can't buy a carton of milk with a million dollars, then there's nothing to do. But I don't believe we're really going to be financially bombed back to the Stone Age, so I think we just go with it. It will get worse, but we ride it out. Fuck it, we hang on."

# TWENTY-EIGHT

Lise checked to see if she had left anything in the bathroom, but she knew she hadn't. She just wanted to stand in the doorway and admire the cleaning job she'd done. The white porcelain was as shiny as the nickel-plated faucets. No stray hairs, everything in its place. Major Beck's wife would be relieved, not just that her husband's house guest was finally leaving, but that she hadn't left a mess.

Lise closed her suitcase and stood it next to the packed duffle and the box of household items she had accumulated—a non-stick fry pan, a rubber spatula, some plastic forks, a Dustbuster, and an electric clock radio. The scene reminded her of helping Sarah and Emily pack up Nina's place. They did it in front of Nina in a way, the box of her bones and ashes sat on the small table while they worked. Lise had felt she was orbiting it the whole afternoon. And then Emily put the box in the messenger bag just before they left and everything felt to Lise as if it was suddenly in its proper place.

Lise packed up the car and drove out of Sierra Madre, taking the 210 to the 134 to the Hollywood Freeway down into Hollywood and then Beverly Hills—feeling like she was getting the hang of all the numbers and the directions, the exits and entrances, the speed at which she was supposed to travel.

The parking structure at the hospital gave her trouble. There were few open spots as she circled, climbing higher and higher, and most of them looked too small even for the Jetta.

She was thirty minutes early for her appointment and tilted the seat back, locking the doors, hoping she could take a quick nap. Sleeping at night was still hard, would likely continue to be hard. The desert hadn't cured her although she hadn't had much hope for that as a remedy. She had managed to sleep while Danny read her the new TV pilot he'd written in a four-day writing binge. He hadn't minded too much, she didn't think. She knew the story anyway. There was a lot of Nik, Maxwell, Acevedo, Nina and Lise in it. There was a character who seemed like Jim, a visitor, who had the same symptoms but not the same disease. And there was a bartender-slash-writer who was a version of Danny, with less cash and fewer shirts. The story made sense to her and she could understand the dialogue, even though it sounded choppy.

The nurse manager of the emergency department was a ripped guy who looked like he worked out two hours each morning. He smiled warmly and talked quietly to Lise, letting her sit in a chair with her back to the wall, with his office door open.

"That's great, I see you've got your ACLS and your PALS," he said, looking down at her paperwork. "The PALS isn't always basic so that's good you have that. And wow, you've got your ATLS. I've heard that is one kick-ass course."

Lise couldn't remember what the letters stood for. "Yeah, I uh, A-T—" Lise tried to grasp the knowledge, but it slipped from her.

The nurse manager's face softened and his eyes widened. "Advanced Trauma Life Support, right?"

Lise got it then. "Yes, ATLS, totally kick-ass. We trained in combat conditions down in Texas."

"Bet it was hot."

"Baghdad was hot. Texas was nothing." She was getting the hang of the banter.

"I know you're familiar working with techs, having been in the military. The ED has a lot of techs from the base down the coast. The techs are terrific, super supportive of the nurses, really great working relationships."

"That's great to hear," Lise said, forgetting why she was talking to this guy.

"You come highly recommended, but I still need to ask the standard interview questions."

"Of course." That's right, Major Beck had set this up, a favor he said, a friend would talk to her.

"Can you describe a difficult experience working in the emergency department? How did you handle it? And looking back now, would you do anything differently?"

Lise listened to the words, hearing them correctly she believed, understanding the sounds and the order in which they were said. This all reminded her of early Danny, the ridiculous questions about good days and bad days in Iraq, the pushing for events to be made neat and tidy for movie screens.

She reached through the Green Zone and back to Denver. She'd made a mistake on a chart, a colleague caught it later, no harm done. She was more careful after that, even asking someone else to look at what she had written for confirmation. As the words came out of Lise, she wondered where the story came from—a shift at St. Anthony North or one of her nursing school text books. It didn't sound real or belonging to her, but it sounded right.

The nurse manager had put Lise's papers in a folder by the time Lise finished speaking.

"Are you okay working nights? Our only openings are on the overnight," he said, moving objects on his desk, tidying up to go home.

"Nights are fine," Lise said because they were.

Walking up the circling inclines of the parking structure, Lise realized that she had failed the interview. She didn't know what question she hadn't answered correctly or what impairment she had failed to cover. She wasn't even sure now how real the interview was. Maybe Major Beck was trying to get her moving in another direction.

She took easy turns in the Jetta, moving with traffic, not forcing herself into lanes, and ended up on Sunset going West straight into the setting sun. Sometimes the road dipped down among the surrounding lush foliage and for a moment it would seem as if the sun had already set. But then the road would turn, rising, and the bleeding orange globe was still visible ahead. Soon she realized she was racing the sun, hoping urgently to get to the beach before it set. The road was twisty, angled oddly around curves and the flow of traffic was fast. There were moments when Lise felt the car slipping from her control, going too fast around a turn, her vision momentarily blinded by glare, her foot pressing the accelerator when she should've hit the break.

She was stopped finally by the traffic light at the Pacific Coast Highway. She had lost. The sky was black. The sun had sunk into the dark ocean ahead of her. She was panting, struggling for a full breath, reaching to steady herself.

## TWENTY-NINE

Jim sat in his seat on the private jet that Mark and Bill had sent. He had spent five days in the hospital and then a week in a hotel, Emily and Sarah helping him too much, the cardiac rehab he attended every day, not helping him enough. He wasn't sure what he wanted from these people or this time in limbo, but he didn't feel he was getting it. He was a stranger again in the world, sad about people he shouldn't care about, anxious about events he had never believed mattered before. Nina's death weighed on him less as the hours went by and the financial collapse—there had to be a better word—occupied his thoughts with increasing dominance.

He was grateful for his friends' extravagant gift—they sent a plane for him! He didn't feel outdone by them, in fact he luxuriated in the gesture. Sarah knew it pleased him and left him alone on the plane with the silent nurse and her equipment, just in case. Sarah sat with Emily, who wanted to order strange things to eat and drink from the flight steward just to see what the jet had on hand. Jim tried to ignore the nurse occasionally taking his pulse and testing his oxygen intake. Maybe they should have taken the train—but he wanted to be home now.

Emily carried Nina's boxed ashes in the messenger bag from the rental house and Jim wanted to stay as far away from that object as possible. He hadn't quizzed Emily or Sarah about the gathering of Nina's belongings or the arrangements with the morgue and the place that had turned her into ashes.

"You okay, babe?" Sarah smiled at him from across the width of the plane.

"Just a little winded," Jim said, although he wasn't, not yet. He knew he would be soon and wanted to get the telling of it out of the way now. The nurse descended on him immediately, checking the parts of him she needed to check.

Each grinding roar of the ascendant airplane's engines made him worry that the change in altitude would rupture his stitches or cause his heart to explode. He saw his blood and flesh all over the beige cabin interior, his daughter and his wife. The nurse would have to clean it all up. The horror movie images disturbed his sleep across the country.

He woke as the plane descended, discovering his fingers tracing the bandages over his incisions. There would be three scars, one two-inches long and the other two one-inch, he had been told. He was savagely dehydrated and gulped at a water bottle, feeling he was staving off death with every drop of liquid. The nurse replaced the water bottle with an oxygen mask. He took a few deep hits, with Sarah and Emily looking at him as if he was the smallest man in the world, and when he felt that all this was more optional than necessary, he handed the oxygen mask back to the nurse.

There was no one to meet them when they landed. No guy with a homemade sign reading "Wicklow." Sarah tried to get mad, yelling into her cell phone, but Jim just shook his head.

"Let's just find a cab," he said. He watched Emily drop her shoulders in relief. Sarah closed her phone and followed him out of the terminal. The nurse was discharged, having returned him safely.

"Business or pleasure?" The driver threw a glance into the rear-view mirror.

Christ, Jim thought. How'd he get the last English-speaking cabbie in New York? He would have much preferred the guy mutter Urdu into his Bluetooth headset all the way into Manhattan.

"You okay?" Sarah asked Jim.

"He's fine," Emily answered for him.

"You in the city for business or pleasure?" The cabbie insisted to Jim.

"I live here," Jim whispered, feeling Emily come alert to a possible change in her dad's life.

"What was that?" The cabbie squawked.

"I live here," Jim said a bit louder, turning his head to look out the window to cut the conversation short. The driver glanced at the group in his rearview mirror and then fell into sullen silence.

Once they were through the tunnel, Jim had the cabbie drop them on Lexington in the 30s. He gave him a big tip, touching the 25% button on the screen. He felt bad about telling him to shut up, and he wanted to spend that money, test the system. And he wanted to walk, test his limits in the city.

Jim ambled slowly up the avenue, Sarah and Emily following him, watching him, bewildered by his behavior but only asking one question: Are you okay? Jim knew he was walking in the right direction, but took his time getting there. The city offered delays and distractions along the way. Emily was glad to go into stores, but Sarah wanted to get him to a couch or a bed. He and Emily ate cookies though he wasn't hungry—he just wanted to buy something, experience the transaction. He retrieved $400 in twenties from an ATM mostly to see if the machine still worked. Sarah and Emily stood in the bank vestibule with him, mystified at his methodical approach to the withdrawal.

"Still working?" Sarah asked as he waited for his receipt. She sounded snippy and impatient to him, but he didn't care.

"Yup, still working," Jim said with a big smile.

"You're excessively amazing, but in a good way," Emily said.

"Not the only one, sweetie," was his reply. "Let's get a cab."

"Finally," said Sarah.

Sarah remained impatient and hovering as they made themselves at home in the New York hotel room. She embraced Jim with comfort and care, asking him how he was feeling, catering to him in a vaguely maternal way. Quickly though her body revealed its edges to him and her administrations became sexual. She sat on the bed, her tongue darted from her mouth into his, and her hands sprouted probing fingers. She put his hand between her thighs. Jim froze. He felt assaulted, panicky. What had the doctor said. Six to eight weeks was all he could remember. He firmly placed her body away from his, releasing her from his hands.

Sarah stared at him, confused, her chest heaving with thwarted energy.

"Six to eight weeks," Jim said. "The heart guy said six to eight weeks."

He watched her face adjust to this as new information. Had he gotten this wrong? Why was she surprised?

"You must be exhausted," she offered. "I'm sorry, you need sleep."

"Let me just nap for an hour. Can you turn on the TV?"

"You going to watch while you sleep?" Sarah thought this was funny, but Jim was entirely serious.

"Put on CNN. It'll seep in while I'm out. I don't want to miss anything."

"Seriously?" Sarah's tone kept shifting on him. He wasn't sure whether to feel loved or laughed at.

Jim slid down from the pillows and rolled into a sleeping position among the sheets. "Don't worry about money," he said as he plunged into sleep.

A day later, all through the memorial service for Nina, Jim thought about his own wrongness, in time and place. The room where they held Nina's memorial service felt like Mars to him. And he couldn't tell if the service was happening too late or too early. Nina had been dead for so long—or was it too soon for her to be gone. And he had not brought a body back to Diana, just a box of ashes. Had he broken another promise?

He sat among Nina's few friends and Diana's swarm of far-flung relatives who had come together—the Wicklows finally out-numbered. Awkward young people stood to speak with logic and clarity and unintentional poetry and returned to their seats to fidget and weep. Emily read from a quavering page of Mariah Carey lyrics. J.J. had still not surfaced from his other obligations. One of Diana's brothers read from a book Jim had never heard of but that everyone else seemed to hold in slack-jawed esteem. An elderly aunt read a poem. How big was this woman's family? Jim thought briefly of Jen—she was part of this kinship network. He was glad she had disappeared after Palm Desert.

He felt the depression pull him in. The cardiologist had warned him, that it would come and go, that it would hang on. He needed to make a plan, acclimate to this alien world that was appar-ently now his home. Get back in the swim of it, do business, earn. This was what he did better, how he could live better. So after the service, when he looked through the restaurant Sarah had chosen for Nina's wake party, and saw Phil Klein shouldering his way through the crowd, he was ready to buy what Phil was selling.

Jim and Phil bellied up to the bar. Phil sucked on ice drowned in Glenlivet and Jim tried to ignore his own incredibly powerful im-pulse to do the same. He hadn't had a drink since Palm Desert. He had no access in the hospital and he had exerted astonishing will power over the mini bars in the hotels. He knew he was off the wag-on, knew he would drink once or twice, or even three times before taking the oath again and never drinking again, again.

"People in your family need to stop dying," Phil said, swallow-ing half the whiskey in his glass. "God bless Ryan and Nina and all the Wicklows." Phil swallowed the rest of the whiskey.

"You sound more like an old Irishman than a middle-age Jew, Philly," Jim said. He hadn't talked like this in years—old school New York back-and-forth, everything on the table while you played it close to the vest, fingers crossed behind your back.

Phil had been his disgruntled number-two guy on his Pruden-tial Bache team back in ancient times—Ryan had smoothed his ruf-fled feathers more than once. Jim had not taken Phil with him when he started his own shop, but Ryan had stayed in touch.

"It's been hard to wrap my head around this," Jim half-feigned the admission while still maintaining his toughness.

"I had to pay my respects today and check in on you. You kind of dropped out of sight. It's one thing to find a new wife and move to the country, but you slid off the face of the earth. Have you checked your Yahoo account the last few years?" Phil had a lot to say.

Jim didn't feel as if he could explain his behavior. He was only just now—gazing at the whiskey drops on Phil's lips—realizing he might have a few unread emails in that Yahoo inbox.

"I had a coronary and triple-bypass less than two weeks ago. A little out of the loop. Doctor says no heavy lifting or checking email for six to eight weeks."

"I had one of those. Double-bypass though," Phil said, look-ing around for the bartender.

"Do you win with more bypass or less?" Jim laughed, partly be-cause he couldn't figure out the answer. "I'm sorry," he added, trying to sound genuine, almost meaning it. "About not staying in touch."

"No you're not." Phil flashed a smile to show he was going to dispense some tough love. "You're just who you are. Fine. I get it. We all took a knee after nine-eleven, but then we got back in the game. Except you."

"I manage my portfolio, keep an eye on my positions. I'm not totally out of it." Jim could feel the offer coming, could feel the deal emerging from Phil's tough-guy niceties. He was his friend after all.

"Rumor is you're raising chickens."

"I kill chickens," said Jim, although it was not entirely true. The thought of their blood made him warm as if he was sinking into sadness. Jim stopped the momentum of the descending depressive mood with sheer grit—and a familiar crutch. He lifted his eyes to the bartender, nodded at him and then glanced at Phil's drink. A duplicate appeared in Jim's hand and he lifted the rock glass to his mouth, tilted it and swallowed the liquid.

Nothing happened except that he didn't die. Had the cardiologist allowed alcohol? He looked around the restaurant. Sarah was sipping a glass of red wine and Cath was taking a second round of something with vodka from a waiter. A couple of young men about J.J.'s age, wearing army wardrobe remnants, were putting their mouths to beer bottles. He thought of Lise, then looked for Emily, but couldn't find her. He rotated his head to face Phil Klein standing in front of him, ordering another for himself and throwing Jim a life preserver.

"Let me help you out with something," Phil offered.

Here comes the deal, Jim thought, taking another sip of the drink he couldn't believe he was drinking.

"We do for each other, right? I'm the only other guy in the world who still knows what CATs were. The old timers need to stick together. These hedge fuckers are killing us and eating their young. And now this crazy shit. You and I both know these credit default swaps aren't the shit show the press has been making them out to be."

Jim took another swallow of the magic elixir and waited patiently for the smart buy he was about to be offered from an old friend so he could feel like he was back in it. Because what he needed was to transact business, to use money, to earn money, to prove himself to himself not by surviving the desert or by keeping an eye on his portfolio or hiding out on the Cape, but by buying and selling.

Jim bought the CDS from Phil for one million dollars while he waited for his second drink to arrive. They clinked glasses, acted like it was no biggie and deliberately did not shake hands. Jim wasn't sure what he was high on: the Glenlivet or the transaction.

In the elevator at the hotel, Jim kissed his wife. He put his tongue in her mouth and thought that six to eight weeks was too long. He suddenly felt capable of the conquering pulse and fearless release of coming inside her body. Just as quickly he was chilled with the thought that fucking her could kill him. He withdrew from her mouth, taking with him the taste of wine, whiskey and fear.

"I'm sorry, babe. I must taste like all that Pinot Noir I was drinking," Sarah said. "I should probably try to be better about that."

Jim wondered if he would ever feel bad about lying to her. He wondered if she could taste his lie now and was just keeping it to herself. "No worries. It's my little cheat." He pulled her closer to him, it was what he would allow himself for now. "All I ever taste is you."

"You're a real smooth talker, James Wicklow Senior," Sarah said.

In the middle of the night, he sat on the floor of the bathroom, his back against the cool wall of tiles, his legs out in front of him, hoping Sarah wouldn't hear him whispering into the phone to the cardiologist on call. Yes, he drank alcohol, yes he ate, yes he was on his feet most of the afternoon and evening, yes he was exhausted. No he was not nauseous, no he had no chest pain or jaw pain or arm pain, no he wasn't sweaty, no he wasn't short of breath, no he did not want to meet at the Lenox Hill ER. He was back in business, he told the doctor, and he wanted to ride it out.

# OCTOBER 4, 2011

Diana Vargas Wicklow sat in her new office, checking to see if anything had been left in the desk drawers that she didn't want. It was only her second week on the job and she still didn't quite feel she belonged in this place again. Not that she wasn't ready, not that she wasn't qualified—there was just that feeling when she didn't think there was enough air in the rooms she moved through. Ultimately it thrilled her, gave her a reason to descend into the subway each day and rise up from under ground ready to put on armor and go to work.

She kept her family photos in a drawer instead of displaying them in the open the way she saw other people do. She wasn't even sure why people had pictures of loved ones at the office. Did they think they would forget them? Or maybe they needed them for constant inspiration, a reminder of why they left them each morning.

She kept pictures of Ryan and Nina in her wallet and at home on one wall. She had digitized all the images and documents she had proving their existence in the world and she clicked through them from time to time, on bright summer Saturdays and dark winter weekday afternoons, but not as much as she had in the autumn Nina had died, when it seemed that clicking a computer mouse was all she had strength for.

In the top desk drawer in the new office, she kept a digital picture frame with rotating images of Ryan and Nina, together and apart. Diana was in none of the photos—she had taken them all. The frame cycled through the eight images in the dark of the drawer, out of sight.

She was supposed to be working out the nursing schedule for the coming week, but she was having a hard time focusing. The television in the waiting room across the hall was playing just a little too loudly. There had been a car bombing in Mogadishu—130 dead—and flooding in Cambodia along the Mekong River—164 dead.

"Can you sign my vacation request for November, please?" One of the nurses stuck her head in the doorway, relieving Diana of her distraction.

"Sure, of course," Diana said, knowing she'd have to start working on the schedules for the rest of the year with the holidays causing chaos. Maybe she'd take extra shifts herself.

Diana signed the form that was put in front of her.

"The universe is expanding," the nurse said as Diana handed back the form.

"What?" Diana smiled, preparing to hear the rest of the joke.

"For real. These guys just won a Nobel Prize for proving the universe is expanding really fast. I heard it on the news just now."

"We need to turn that TV down," Diana said. "You're learning way too much."

Their laughter was interrupted by another nurse, breathless, moving past the open door.

"Helicopter crash East River. Multiple casualties coming to us," she said and was gone.

Diana felt the familiar rushing urgency rise in her. She controlled it and converted it into something calm and useful.

"Let's get ready," she said.

Diana walked the long hallway of the emergency department, watching as nurses and doctors prepared themselves and the equipment. She walked out through the sliding doors onto the sidewalk of the ambulance bay. The moment reminded her of September 11th, when she had stood outside the emergency entrance of St. Vincent's with her colleagues, dressed in scrubs, their hands resting on every rolling chair they could find, each chair wrapped in blue sterile sheets, waiting for the victims that never came.

She heard the approaching sirens and waited for the wounded to arrive.

## ACKNOWLEDGMENTS

I want to thank reporters for the *New York Times* and the *Los Angeles Times* for their informative and insightful coverage of the U.S. wars in Afghanistan and Iraq, combat veterans returning home and the events of the 2008 financial crisis.

The National Institute of Mental Health and the U.S. Department of Veterans Affairs provided excellent information on PTSD, as did the book *Trauma and Recovery* by Judith Herman, M.D.

I want to give a very loud shout-out to the makers of the award-winning documentary *Baghdad ER*. Thank you for telling the stories of the nurses and doctors of the 86th Combat Support Hospital in the Green Zone in Baghdad.

I have wonderful friends and family who were more than willing to educate me about things I didn't know. Thanks to my sister Sally Dreslin (heart attacks and all things medical), Kevin Flaherty (financial markets), Tamar Haspel (Rhode Island Reds and all things Cape Cod), and Lisa Quiñonez (Sierra Madre and the desert). These folks know their stuff and all errors here are mine.

Thank you to the faculty and students at The New School in New York where I recently completed a M.A. in Liberal Studies. I could not have written this book without living and learning in your company. A special thanks to Professor Melissa Monroe who re-introduced me to *The Odyssey*, another story of a very long journey home.

Thank you to the team at C&R Press, especially publishers, John Gosslee and Andrew Sullivan, as well as copyeditor extraordinaire, Andrew Hachey, who untangled some of my sentences.

Thank you to my writing workshop colleagues, Susan Buttenweiser, Carolyn Goldhush, Bernard Lumpkin and Jason Lees. You gave me really helpful feedback, asked tough questions and offered community and support.

I want to thank (and thank and thank and thank) John Reed—writer, editor, teacher and generous fairy godfather who always helped me find my literary mojo when I thought I'd lost it. This book exists because you told me I could write it.

Thank you to old and new (and some late) friends who have cheered me on and supported my writing: Lisa Quiñonez, Dana Michel, Sharon Merle-Lieberman, John Wolfarth, Jackie Duvoisin, Tamar Haspel, Marsha Seeman, Susan Shapiro, Jennifer Bassett, Ingrid Uribe, Justin Nuttall, Ryan Fox, Keisha Bush, Patrick Ryan, Craig Anderson, Roger Robinson, Joe Lagana, Clyde Lieberman, Kate Levinson, Paul Smalera, Anna Schachner, Christopher Schnieders, Joseph Salvatore, Brian Hurley, Patricia Craig, Trudy Hale, Simmons Buntin, Hugh Nissenson and John Ford.

Thank you to my mother, Anne Rogin, and the rest of my family, especially to my father Richard Rogin and my uncle Gilbert Rogin—both writers. I was born to this work, but you showed me how difficult and delightful the writer's life can be.